Greg................................**for**
wake..................................**ck**

Co.................................... **Y**
midn

Silence fe...
shoulders to...
a scraping o............corridor, a ...... then ...., and…
If he didn't know better he would have said that the
clatter was the sound of chains.

Greg was suddenly awake, his eyes straining in the
darkness—and then clamped shut as white light
suddenly hit his retinas, burning the outline of a
shadowy figure into his mind's eye.

'Greg!'

'What…? Jess…?'

He blinked against the light streaming in through the
open door and slowly began to make her out. She
had on the same red coat that she'd been wearing
when he'd seen her last. His mouth went dry. *When
he'd seen her last…*

When he'd seen her last he'd been kissing her.

The length of chain slung over her shoulder and
trailing behind her on the floor was new, and
she hadn't been quite so grimy then either. The
temptation to reach out and touch her, pretend she
had a smudge on her cheek so that he could wipe it
away, was almost irresistible.

Dear Reader

Since the earliest times people have gathered together and told each other stories. Stories about things they've seen or done, funny stories, sad stories, tales with a moral to them. In the times when books were only available to the very privileged few storytelling was a way of passing on knowledge and experience, of sharing and understanding who we are.

And Christmas is a time for storytelling. It's a way of looking back, making sense of the past, of looking at our lives now and giving us direction for the future. No wonder *Once upon a time…* are four of the most powerful and magical words in our language.

Jess Saunders shares my own love of storytelling, and when she's put in charge of the hospital's Christmas pageant it's one of the things that she's bound to include. Inspired by *A Christmas Carol* by Charles Dickens, she's determined to make this year one to remember—but she's not prepared for how this wonderful story might touch her own life.

Thank you for sharing Greg and Jess's story with me. I always love to hear from readers, and you can contact me via my website at www.annieclaydon.com

Annie

ONCE UPON A CHRISTMAS NIGHT…

BY
ANNIE CLAYDON

MILLS &
BOON

First published in Great Britain 2013
by Mills & Boon, an imprint of Harlequin (UK) Limited.
Harlequin (UK) Limited, Eton House,
18-24 Paradise Road, Richmond, Surrey TW9 1SR

© Annie Claydon 2013

ISBN: 978 0 263 89929 0

Harlequin (UK) policy is to use papers that are natural, renewable
and recyclable products and made from wood grown in sustainable
forests. The logging and manufacturing process conform to the
legal environmental regulations of the country of origin.

Printed and bound in Spain
by Blackprint CPI, Barcelona

Cursed from an early age with a poor sense of direction and a propensity to read, **Annie Claydon** spent much of her childhood lost in books. After completing her degree in English Literature, she indulged her love of romantic fiction and spent a long, hot summer writing a book of her own. It was duly rejected and life took over. A series of U-turns led in the unlikely direction of a career in computing and information technology, but the lure of the printed page proved too much to bear, and she now has the perfect outlet for the stories which have always run through her head, writing Medical Romance™ for Mills & Boon®. Living in London, a city where getting lost can be a joy, she has no regrets for having taken her time in working her way back to the place that she started from.

Recent titles by Annie Claydon:

RE-AWAKENING HIS SHY NURSE
THE REBEL AND MISS JONES
THE DOCTOR MEETS HER MATCH
DOCTOR ON HER DOORSTEP
ALL SHE WANTS FOR CHRISTMAS

To Cassie and George, with much love.

CHAPTER ONE

GREG SHAW OPENED the door of the doctors' common room, not bothering to switch on the light, and slung himself into a chair. All he wanted was sleep. He could have done with a few days off in between returning from America and resuming his job, but what you wanted wasn't always what you got. A day to get over the jet lag, unpack and re-stock the larder hadn't been enough and he'd had to satisfy himself with doing none of those things with any degree of completeness.

He should go home. Catch some sleep before he was due back on shift again tomorrow. He tried to work up enough enthusiasm to propel himself into action by promising himself a hot shower and a cooked meal, but the relief of sitting here alone outweighed all of that at the moment. In the darkness, he was hardly aware of the fact that his eyes were closing.

'Is it always so hot in here?' Jessie Saunders picked her way down the steep concrete steps, which seemed to lead directly into a sauna.

'No idea. Apparently the quickest way through is via the boiler room.' Reena was having to shout now, to make herself heard over the din. 'Watch out for that handrail, it wobbles terribly.'

'So it's fair to assume that Health and Safety haven't been down here recently.'

'Probably not.' Reena shot her a grin and led the way through to the far door, which gave way to a cooler, quieter corridor. 'The hospital records should be through there.'

The records room, as the notice on the door grandly announced, turned out to be a long, low-ceilinged vault, filled with row upon row of shelves. Reena felt in the pocket of her coat and consulted a piece of paper. 'Right, so the early stuff's over there in the far corner.' She pulled a large, old-fashioned key from her pocket and indicated a heavy metal door.

'What's that? I didn't know we had dungeons in the basement.'

'It's an old walk-in safe. It's cool and dry so they keep the earlier documents in there. I had to promise Administration that we'd wedge the door open and keep the key with us at all times.'

'And they know we're down here this late?' There was no reason for the basement to feel any darker or spookier now than it would have done at lunchtime. Somehow it did.

'I said we were going to have a look after work. They might have thought that was five-thirty.' Reena unlocked the door, pulling it back with an effort and wedging it firmly.

Jess shrugged, pulling a couple of pairs of surgical gloves from her pocket. 'Gloves?'

'Definitely.'

The boxes of papers stacked inside might be caked with dust, but they were stored in some sort of order. The year 1813 was located and the boxes pulled out into the cramped space outside the door.

'Oh, you'll never guess who I saw coming out of the canteen today.' Reena was carefully sifting through the contents of the oldest storage box, trying not to disturb too much dust.

'No, I don't think I will.'

'Give it a go, at least. Great smile.'

'The tooth fairy?'

'Ha-ha. Think taller. Darker and not wearing a tutu.' Reena rolled her eyes when Jess gave her a blank look. 'Your ex-boss.'

'You mean…' It would be disingenuous to pretend that she didn't know who Reena meant. 'Greg? He's back?'

Breathing would be good right now, but Jess's lungs seemed to have temporarily forgotten how. She kept her eyes firmly fixed on the large ledger in front of her so they couldn't betray her shock.

'Yeah. Wherever he's been for the last eight months, he's been getting some sun. He's looking good.'

Greg always looked good. Jess wondered whether Reena had any more substantive information and how she was going to ask for it without sounding too interested. 'So how is he?'

'I didn't see him to speak to, he was moving too fast for that.' Reena tossed her head and laughed. 'You know Greg. He's a busy kind of guy.' She turned her attention back to the half empty storage box.

He was back. He'd probably had two or three girlfriends since Jess had seen him last and had almost certainly forgotten all about That Kiss. Just the way she should have done.

'This looks promising… Jess?'

'Uh?'

'I think this is exactly what we're looking for.'

'Yeah?' Jess straightened, shrugging off the brief scrap of memory, which seemed to have lodged itself right in the centre of her consciousness. 'Let's have a look.'

* * *

Greg drifted into what passed for wakefulness in time to hear the clock in the small courtyard outside the common-room window chiming out midnight. Silence fell, and he sat up straight, easing his shoulders to iron out a few of the kinks. There was a scraping outside in the corridor, a dull thud and... If he didn't know better he would have said that the clatter was the sound of chains.

Leave it out. After eight months, spent jetting around America and Australia, with some of the sunnier parts of Europe thrown in, London in early November seemed claustrophobic, full of shadows. But it was home. He'd longed to be back home, and now here he was. Feeling just as empty and unsure as he had for the last ten months.

Another clatter. If it wasn't a chain, it was something that sounded pretty much identical. Greg was suddenly awake, his eyes straining in the darkness, and then clamped shut as white light hit his retinas, burning the outline of a shadowy figure into his mind's eye.

'Greg!'

'What...? Jess?' He blinked against the light streaming in through the open door and slowly began to make her out. She had on the same red coat that she'd been wearing when he'd seen her last. His mouth went dry. When he'd seen her last...

When he'd seen her last he'd been kissing her. The length of chain, slung over her shoulder and trailing behind her on the floor, was new, and she hadn't been quite so grimy then either. The temptation to reach out and touch her, pretend she had a smudge on her cheek so that he could wipe it away, was almost irresistible.

She was staring at him as if she'd just seen a ghost. She swallowed hard and seemed to come to her senses. 'I heard you were back.'

'Yeah. Only just. I landed yesterday morning, and got a call at lunchtime, saying that they were short-staffed in A and E and could I start work today.' Guilt trickled down his spine. He probably should have called her. He'd thought about it often enough.

She nodded. No hint in her steady gaze that their kiss figured anywhere in her attitude towards him. 'Well, it's nice to see you back. Have you got…things…settled?'

'Not quite.' It was never going to be completely settled. 'For the time being.' The urge to explain himself was prickling at the back of Greg's neck, but he had no idea where to start. 'Jess…'

'Yes?'

'What's with the chains?'

She flushed prettily. Dragged the knitted beret off her head, leaving her honey-coloured hair impossibly rumpled. A little longer than it had been last Christmas, and the style suited her.

'Ah.' She started to unwind the length of chain from her neck. 'It's for the dressing up. For Christmas.' She indicated a stack of plastic crates in the corner.

'You're going to dress up in chains for Christmas?' Greg couldn't help smiling and she shot him a glare in return.

'No, of course not. Gerry is.' She finally managed to free herself from the chain, opening one of the crates and dumping it inside.

'Gerry's going to dress up in chains for Christmas?' Gerard Mortimer, the senior cardiac consultant. Greg was sure that there were plenty of things more incongruous in the world, but at the moment he couldn't bring any of them to mind. 'Starting when?'

This time her look was ferocious enough to have cut through cold steel. 'Some of us are dressing up as characters from Dickens's novels. Gerry's going to be Jacob Marley's ghost.'

There were no words to say. Greg began to wonder whether he wasn't dreaming after all. It wouldn't have been the first time that Jess had featured in his dreams, but he had to admit that the chains were a new development. Maybe fatigue was lending an edge to his imagination.

'Are you okay?' She was staring at him intently.

'Uh…?' On the off chance that he was dealing with reality and not a set of unconnected threads from his unconscious mind, he should give an answer of some sort. 'Yeah, fine. Jet lag. So who are you dressing up as?' It couldn't hurt to ask, and Greg found that he was suddenly and irrationally interested.

'I'm not dressing up. I'm organising everything.'

'So this Christmas won't be as chaotic as last…' He bit his tongue but it was too late. The cat had clawed its way out of the bag and ushered something that looked suspiciously like an elephant into the room.

'I don't know what you mean.'

She was blushing furiously, refusing to meet his gaze. She remembered. And from the look of things she was no more indifferent to it than he was. Greg could barely suppress his grin.

'I meant that…the weather will probably be better.'

'Yes. I expect so. Last year was quite unusual.' She was backing towards the door now. 'It's late. I'd better be getting home.'

'See you tomorrow?'

'Yes… Maybe.'

'I'll look forward to it.' The door banged behind her, and Greg settled back into his chair. Just another ten minutes, to settle his jumbled thoughts, then he'd go home.

Last Christmas...

The dream seized Greg with all the colour and immediacy of a memory, which had shadowed him for the last thirty years. The large, opulent room and the child, sitting on a thick, intricately patterned rug on the floor.

He was making something. Without having to look, Greg knew what it was. The Christmas card was for his father, the picture on the front a wishful representation of a family—father, mother and their five-year-old son— under a Christmas tree. It was almost painful to watch his younger self, so absorbed in this task, so careful with the picture and the wording inside the card, because Greg knew what was to come.

The lavishly wrapped presents from America had been no substitute for his father's arrival, but the child had believed all the excuses that Christmas. It had taken years of broken promises to finally squash Greg's faith and make him realise that the time his father gave so freely to the company and the people he worked with was doled out like a miser's shilling to his family.

'It's not your fault.' Greg breathed the words to his younger self, wondering if there was any way he could comfort the boy. Apparently not. His own memories still tasted of the bitterness of dreams that had never been smashed but had just dissolved under the weight of reality.

The boy was growing, though, almost before his eyes. Finding his way in the world. A first kiss on a sun-strewn hillside in Italy, where he had been holidaying with his mother's family. The letter to his father, telling him that he was going to medical school, which had gone unanswered. The party that his mother and stepfather had thrown for him before he'd left home. The hard work, the weary nights and the smile of a woman he'd saved. She'd been the first,

*and from then on he'd known that this was what he was
supposed to do.*

*Greg was reeling from the vivid clarity of the thoughts
and memories flashing in front of him. Faces, dreams. The
soft touch of a woman's skin. Jess. She'd been the last, delicious taste of the life that he'd left behind. Maybe not a
perfect life, there had been the usual mistakes, the usual
disappointments, but it had been his and he had a singu-
lar affection for it.*

*Finally, the parade of images slowed. Stopped. It was
last Christmas, in the dark, deserted courtyard outside
the hospital, and Greg could see himself, talking to Jess.
Although he couldn't hear what they were saying, he knew
well enough. Knew what was coming, too, and he held his
breath, afraid that in some way he might alter history and
divert their path away from that sweet outcome.*

*She must have been as back-breakingly tired as he was,
but she still shone. Still wore that red sparkly headband
that had brought a little Christmas cheer into an A and E
department that had been in a state of siege after a cold
snap, accompanied by snow, had filled the waiting room,
and a flu bug had thrown the holiday rota into chaos.*

*Greg saw himself grimace. They'd got to the goodbye.
Jess had worked for him for two years, and was leaving
soon, to take up a post in Cardiology. It was what she
wanted to do and he was pleased for her but even now,
ten months later, the sudden feeling of loss stabbed at him.*

*There it was... Greg watched as his former self leaned
forward, a brief kiss on the cheek. Saw her flinch back in
surprise as he went to kiss the other cheek, and knew that
he'd whispered something about a single kiss not being
enough, using his Italian heritage as an excuse for his own
craving to feel her skin against his again.*

More talk, their bodies seeming to grow closer by the

second, and then he'd caught her hand. Pressed her fingers against his lips, smiling when she didn't draw back. And then Greg had heedlessly trashed the first of the three rules he'd lived by up until that moment. He'd gone ahead and kissed her, despite the fact that Jess was still a member of his team for another week, and he always, whatever the circumstances, kept it strictly professional at work.

'Think you're in control of this, don't you?'

He murmured the warning and his former self took no heed of it. Jess would show him differently, any minute now. Greg watched as she pulled away for a moment and then kissed him back, her hand sliding over the stubble on his jaw and coming to rest on his neck, in the exact place that had suddenly and inexplicably seemed to control the whole of his body.

She'd torn his breath away, taken everything that he was and made it hers. What was the second rule again? Don't let your love life get out of control? That had dissolved in the wash of pleasure that had been engulfing him, without anything more than a slight pop. This had been uncharted territory. He'd known no more about Jess's personal life than she had about his, and if that wasn't out of control he didn't know what was.

It was Jess who had come to her senses. Down-to-earth, dependable Jess, who had always seemed so immune to his charm.

'This might not be such a good idea. We work together...'

She'd given him a way out, and he'd stubbornly refused to take it.

'Not for much longer.'

'I suppose I won't be seeing so much of you after next week. When I take up the post in Cardiology.'

There had been a gleam of mischief in her smile.

The third rule had flared and burned in the heat of her touch. Don't make promises you can't keep.

'You'll see me. I'll find you.'

He had kissed her one last time, just to let her know that he would. And she had clung to him, to let him know just what his welcome would be like when he did.

'Happy Christmas, Greg.'

'Happy Christmas, Jess.'

Greg's eyes opened and he found himself staring at the ceiling. He hadn't even looked for her, let alone found her. In the week between Christmas and the New Year the call had come, telling him that his father was gravely ill. Instead of going to Jess's goodbye drinks, Greg had been on the motorway, on his way to his father's house. Too late, he'd realised that he'd left no message to tell her why he couldn't be there.

Days had turned into weeks. Every moment that Greg hadn't been at work had been spent either on the road or at his father's bedside. He'd known that he was dying, but somehow it had seemed all wrong when the man who had capitulated to no one gave way to death. Then the will had been read, and Greg's world had been turned upside down. He'd packed his bags and gone to America to try and sort it all out, knowing that it was too late to seek her out.

Maybe she'd forgiven him. She certainly hadn't forgotten him. And maybe now he could do what he'd neglected to do before, and had been regretting for the last ten months. Get to know Jess. Find out whether that kiss had been just an aberration, something that had happened which had never been meant to be, or whether it might, just might have been the start of something.

CHAPTER TWO

GREG BREEZED INTO Cardiology as if it was the most natural thing in the world, and he was simply looking for something he'd misplaced.

'Ah! Just what I needed.' The coffee that he'd bought for Jess was whipped from his hand, and Gerry lifted the take-away cup to his lips.

Best brazen it out. 'Thought you might.' Greg leaned against the reception desk and opened his own coffee.

'So, welcome to Cardiology. And who might you be?' Gerry's Irish accent was always broader when he was smiling.

'Feeling neglected, are we?'

'Not me.' Gerry tipped the coffee cup towards him as if in a toast. 'I'm easily pleased, though. Maura wants to know when you'll be coming over for dinner.'

'Soon. I'm on lates at the moment. But I can pop in at the weekend, see the kids. I've something for them from America.' Something that his father's personal assistant had procured from the toy store. Greg hadn't needed to ask whether Pat had done the same each time his own birthday or Christmas had rolled around. The meticulously wrapped presents for Jamie and Emma bore the same careful folds that he'd examined and practised himself as a child, thinking that this, at least, would be something he'd learned from his father.

'….last time. By the time Jamie's old enough for that remote-controlled car you sent him, I'll have worn it out.' Gerry's voice filtered back into his consciousness.

'I thought you'd like it. And I've got something a bit more age appropriate this time.' Greg would rewrap the parcels himself. Then at least he'd know what was inside them. 'I had some help in choosing. My father's PA is great with things like that.' He'd always loved his presents and had no reason to suppose that Pat had lost her touch. As long as the kids were happy, did it really make so much of a difference?

'Yeah? How are things going over there? You weren't exactly communicative when we spoke last time.'

'I know. It's complicated.'

Gerry bared his teeth in a wry smile. 'What, there's a woman involved?'

'What makes you say that?'

'That's generally your definition of complicated.'

'Never make assumptions.' Greg wondered what kind of rumours had been circulating about his protracted absence. Went as far as hoping that Jess hadn't heard them and then decided not to go there. 'Is Jess around?'

'I think she's doing a ward round.' Gerry flipped an enquiring look at the receptionist, who nodded. 'She'll be back soon. Can I help?'

'Not unless you're in charge of the Christmas pageant.' Gerry wouldn't question the excuse. Jess wasn't 'his type'. It occurred to Greg that perhaps it was the women he usually dated who weren't his type.

'So she's got you involved with that, has she?'

'Not yet. I thought I might lend a hand, though. Anything that involves you in chains has got to be worth a look.'

Gerry chuckled. 'Yeah. Think I got lumbered there.' Something caught his eye and he gestured. 'Jess. You've got a new recruit.'

By the time Greg had turned, her initial reaction to his presence, if indeed there had been one, was under control. He'd never seen her in anything other than scrubs or jeans before, but today she wore a skirt and blouse under her crisp white coat. Hair tied back, showing off the curve of her neck, and, though it came as no particular surprise to Greg that Jess had legs, somehow he couldn't drag his eyes away from them.

'Don't eye my staff up, mate.' At least Gerry had the grace to lean in close so no one else could hear him. Greg shot him a warning look, and Gerry laughed, turning to the receptionist, who immediately gave him something else to do.

'You want to help with the pageant?' Jess's voice next to him was uncertain.

'Oh. Yeah, I thought if you wanted a hand…' He stopped. Suddenly it seemed crass to just breeze in, as if the last ten months hadn't happened.

'Yes. Always.' She twisted her mouth. 'Greg, I… It was such a surprise to see you last night, and I didn't…' She took a breath. 'I just wanted to say that I heard about your father. I'm very sorry. I should have made sure that I got the chance to say that before now.'

He stared at her. He'd left her hanging, without a word, and she was the one who seemed to feel she had something to explain. 'Thanks. And…I was the one who wasn't around, not you.'

'That's understandable.' Suddenly they weren't talking about his father any more. It was all about Greg and Jess.

And that kiss. No, not the kiss, that had been just fine. The promise he'd made and then broken.

'You think so?' Calling her, from his father's place or long distance from America, had seemed somehow indefinably wrong. Now he was back in London, it felt wrong that he hadn't.

She shrugged. 'I'll give you the benefit of the doubt.'

That was all he needed. 'Well, in that case, do you want to meet up? To talk about the pageant, I mean. I could buy you lunch perhaps.'

She pursed her lips. 'You might like to reconsider that. I can think of a lot of jobs in the time it takes to eat lunch. Maybe just a coffee.'

He wanted so badly to push her, not to take no for an answer. But he didn't have the right. Thinking about her for the whole of the last ten months didn't count as any form of contact, unless she happened to be psychic. 'Whatever suits you. Would you like me to call you?'

She nodded, pulling her phone out of her pocket. 'What's your number?'

She thumbed in the digits as he recited them and his mobile sounded, one ring from his back pocket. 'There, you've got mine now. If you want to risk lunch, I'll make a list of things we need help with.'

He grinned. Jess had come through for him yet again. This time he wouldn't let her down.

Are you free for lunch on Sunday?

Jess wasn't about to admit that those seven words were the ones that she'd been waiting for ever since she'd last seen Greg. She texted back with the minimum of information.

Yes.

Come over to mine. I'll make lunch. You can give me a rundown on what you want me to do.

'Don't tempt me...' She hissed the words between her teeth, but couldn't help smiling to herself. He might have left her hanging, and it might have hurt, but Jess wasn't quite sure what she would have done if he hadn't. If Greg had come knocking on her door, she might just have taken fright and pretended she wasn't home.

Sounds good. What time?

I'll pick you up at twelve.

No, that was one step too far for the moment.

Send me your address. I'll make my own way.

There was a pause, and then her phone beeped again. His address, along with an electronic smile. Nothing like his real smile. Good. It was far too early to start thinking about all the things his smile did to her.

The climb up to the top floor wasn't anywhere near long enough to make her feel dizzy, but then Greg answered the door. A blue shirt, open just far enough to show improbably smooth, olive skin and jeans that fitted him like a glove. Dark hair, and dark eyes, which were even more striking here than in the fluorescent glare of the hospital. Couldn't he give a girl a break?

'That smells fabulous. What is it?' When she followed him through to the large, sleek kitchen, the smell curled around her like a warm, comfortable blanket.

'One of my mother's secret recipes.' Greg had clearly

come to the same conclusion that Jess had. The easy humour they'd shared at work was the best way to forget that they were alone together in his flat. 'You know the score. If I tell you what's in there, I...'

'Yeah, I know. You have to shoot me.'

'Yep. Or challenge you to a duel.'

'You prefer hand-to-hand fighting?'

'Every time.' He surveyed the pans on the stove, gave one a stir and then turned his attention back to her. 'Don't you like to be able to look straight into the other man's eyes?'

'Of course. How else would I know exactly what he was thinking?'

He barked out a sudden laugh. 'Touché. So tell me all about this Christmas extravaganza of yours.'

It wasn't really hers and it wasn't much of an extravaganza, but it was something to talk about over their meal. Greg chuckled when she told him about the plan for carol singers, dressed up as characters from Dickens, and loved the idea for storytellers in the children's wards.

'That's a great idea. Aren't you going to go through to the general wards as well?'

'I don't know.' Jess shrugged. 'I didn't really think of doing that.'

'Adults love to be read to as well. There's evidence to suggest that it's beneficial for stroke patients. I imagine that a good storyteller could capture a lot of interest with the elderly as well.'

'Hmm. Yeah, worth thinking about.' She should have known that Greg would be able to add something to the value of the project.

'So what else?'

'As it's the hospital's two hundredth anniversary this year, we're going to do a small exhibition in the main foyer.

How things were then. There are loads of old documents in the basement, and I was thinking of making a model of the building.' He was giving her the same look that everyone gave her when she got to this bit. 'It's not as crazy as it sounds. It's going to be done properly, I'm not thinking of just gluing a couple of empty cereal packets together. It'll be 1:87 scale, like the model trains.'

'Trains?'

Jess rolled her eyes. 'What is it about men and model trains? Yes, trains if you like, the railway ran past the hospital then as well. Only I can't find anyone who's got any trains.'

'I'll give someone a ring. One of my father's associates in America. She has a talent for getting anything you can think of.'

'We don't have a budget…'

He swept her objections away with a wave of his hand. 'That's okay. No budget needed. Pat has a talent for that as well.'

Jess eyed him suspiciously, but he didn't look as if he was going to come up with any further explanations. And she wasn't in a position to look a gift horse in the mouth. 'Thanks. That would be great.' In for a penny… 'And the model?'

His lips twisted into a smile. 'Yeah, okay. I'll sort that out too.' He put his fork down onto his empty plate with a clatter. 'Anything else?'

'No, I think that's enough to keep you busy. Or…Pat, was it?'

He grinned. Perhaps she had been a little too transparent. 'Yeah, Pat. I've known her since I was five years old. She was going to retire this year but I convinced her to stay on for a little while, to help me sort out my father's estate.'

'Oh. Good idea.' Jess wasn't even going to admit to herself that she would have been jealous if Pat had turned out to be a leggy blonde. Or, more exactly, a leggy blonde in her twenties. 'Was it very complicated, then?'

'Yes.' The sudden flatness of his tone said that Greg had divulged as much as he was going to on the subject. 'Did you enjoy your food?'

'Very much. You have a great apartment, too.'

He looked around, as if he hadn't noticed. 'Glad you like it.'

What wasn't to like? Greg didn't live ostentatiously, but all his furniture matched and it screamed quality. And that was before you counted the large, top-floor living space, the tall windows and the amazing view.

'You moved in here recently?' This kind of apartment was far beyond the reach of a doctor's salary. He must have inherited the money from his father.

'No.' He laughed at her surprise. 'I had a trust fund. By the time it matured, it was enough for this place.'

Jess almost choked on the last mouthful from her plate. Greg obviously came from a very different background from hers. 'That sounds...useful.'

He leaned towards her. 'The last time I saw you look that disapproving was when Ray Harris ended up as a patient in his own ambulance.'

'That was my professional face.'

'No, it wasn't. You looked as sour as a bowl of lemons.' He was teasing her now.

'Well, it was a bit much. Ray was just trying to help—the guy didn't need to take a swing at him. How hard do you have to hit someone to break their cheekbone?'

'Hard. And you were a model of restraint. I couldn't have done better myself.' He chuckled.

'Of course you couldn't. I was there, remember? I saw what you did to that drinks machine.'

'It wasn't working. I pressed the button and got hot water all over my feet.'

'You didn't press it, you punched it.'

They were both laughing now. This was almost unbearable. The highs and lows, the humour, the camaraderie, all of it free of the framework of hospital rules and common sense, which had kept their relationship on a professional footing. There was nothing to protect her now.

'So what's so bad about having a trust fund, then?' He was still grinning.

Jess shrugged. 'Thought I was off the hook with that one.'

'You're not on any hook. I'm just interested.'

'I've just never known anyone with a trust fund. Does it make a difference? To the way you look at things, I mean.'

He threaded his fingers together. Long fingers. She already knew that Greg had a sensitive touch. 'I had to work just as hard as everyone else at med school. Lived in the same sorts of digs. It matured when I was thirty and by that time I'd already earned what I really wanted out of life. I imagine that was just as my father intended.'

'He sounds like an astute man.'

Something flickered in his eyes and then died. She was evidently not about to hear any of Greg's thoughts on his father. He rose and collected the empty plates from the table. 'Go and sit down. I'll make some coffee.'

'I'll help you with the dishes.' Jess made to get up.

'My guests don't do washing up.' He grinned at her protest. 'Neither do I. I'm just going to stack these in the dishwasher.'

Right. Of course he was. Jess shook her head at her own lack of sophistication and obediently descended the three steps that divided the dining area from the living space, sitting down on one of the butter-smooth, leather sofas.

He was back in ten minutes, along with a tray, laden with coffee and after-dinner sweets. 'This is nice. Really nice. Thank you.' He was more than just a good cook, he was a good host. Everything was in the right place, at the right time. And Jess was pretty sure that the music playing softly in the background had been chosen with her own favourite tracks in mind.

'Thank you.' He seemed about to ask something and then hesitated.

'I can only say no.' Jess might not have the sophistication that Greg had, but she could read between the lines.

'Nah. You won't do that.' He settled back in his seat, the soft leather easing with him.

'I might. You think you can just charm me into anything?' He probably could, but letting him know that would be a bad move right now.

He thought for a moment. 'No, I don't.' He let the compliment, if that's what it was, sink in. 'Unfortunately.'

'Why unfortunately?'

'Because some things are a lot easier when you have a friend around.'

All right. He'd got her now. After that, she couldn't say no. 'What things?'

'I've inherited a house from my father. I need to go up there next weekend as there are some things I need to sort out. I'd really appreciate some company.'

Jess pressed her burning cheek against the cool, brushed steel wall of the lift. So Greg had secrets. That was okay, everyone had one or two. His family had money. That wasn't exactly his fault. As a colleague, even as a friend, that wouldn't have mattered one way or the other.

He wasn't either of those any more, though. Not quite a lover yet, but Jess was becoming acutely aware that it would only take one touch. One kiss, and this time nothing would be able to stop them.

And if they didn't stop? If they went ahead? Greg would have the power to tip her well-ordered life on its head. Jess had no doubt whatsoever that he would, that was what Greg was like, he thought outside the box. The scariest thing about it was that this only made him even more irresistible.

She sighed. There was no guarantee that he wouldn't transform her world and then leave. If the hospital grapevine was anything to go by, that's exactly what he would do. But that didn't matter any more. However many reasons there were to have nothing more to do with Greg, she was going with him next weekend. That was all there was to it.

CHAPTER THREE

JESS'S WARDROBE WASN'T large, but it was focussed. Plain skirts and trousers and an assortment of matching blouses for work. A tailored suit for interviews, a few pairs of jeans, ranging from new to falling to pieces, and tops, ranging from very warm to very summery. A dress, bought for a summer wedding, which she'd worn only once. Nothing seemed suitable for a visit to the house that Greg had inherited from his father, which sounded large—no, sprawling—and far grander than anything she was used to.

Going out and buying something might have been an option, but she felt unequal to the task. New clothes would only serve to make her feel more uncomfortable anyway. Taking a little more care with her hair and make-up and choosing favourite pieces from her wardrobe would have to be enough.

'You look nice. I like your scarf.' He grinned as he took her coat and weekend bag, opening the passenger door of his car for her.

It was the one thing she'd allowed herself to buy. A pretty lilac scarf that went with her plain grey trousers and sweater and the black leather jacket that she normally kept for best. Greg was wearing jeans and a warm, slightly battered, leather jacket but he had a knack of making scruffy look stylish. Sexy too, but Jess was trying not to think too much about that.

'Do you want to put your jacket in the back? It's a long drive.' Greg had taken his own off and slung it on the back seat before getting into the car.

'Yes. Thanks.' She shrugged out of her jacket and he took it, draping it carefully over his.

'Right, then.' He twisted the key in the ignition. 'Let me know if you get cold and I'll turn the heat up.'

By the time they reached the suburbs she was feeling hot and cold by turn. When they hit the motorway, her stomach began to lurch. What was she doing? She'd been so brave, so thoughtless in agreeing to come away with him. He was so much more than a nice guy and a good doctor. He was sophisticated, drop-dead gorgeous and far more than a girl like her could handle. She was sure to make a fool of herself.

'You okay?'

'Hmm? Yes, fine.' Jess turned her head away from him, staring at the hard shoulder of the motorway.

'Sure?'

Cold perspiration began to form on the side of her brow. Suddenly she felt trapped, carried inexorably towards goodness only knew what. 'Um. Actually, I do feel a little sick.'

'Did you have breakfast this morning?'

She hadn't had time. She had been too busy fussing over her packing and her appearance and stressing about her trip with Greg. 'Not really…'

'There's motorway services a mile up ahead. We'll stop there.'

Just to swell the small fountain of misery that was bubbling up inside her chest, he helped her out of the car when they parked. And because standing made her head swim, she allowed him to. He kept hold of her until she was seated in the corner of the bleak, utilitarian cafeteria and then hurried to fetch toast and two cups of tea.

'Feeling better?' An awkward silence had only been rendered slightly more acceptable by having something to eat and drink.

'Yes. I'm fine, just one of those stupid things.'

He gave the throw-away line rather more consideration that it deserved. 'I could try acupressure.'

'Since when have you done acupressure?' Suddenly there was something to talk about. Something they shared. 'Don't tell me you've been getting into alternative medicine.'

He grinned. 'Don't tell me you've been getting into labels. There are lots of interesting techniques out there that bear quantitative investigation. When I was in the States, I met a guy who uses it to very good effect, in tandem with drug regimes.'

'So you were working as a doctor in America?'

'Just taking an interest.' He steered deftly around the question. 'Here, give me your arm.'

'What, so you can experiment on me? In a café at motorway services?'

'Well, I wouldn't do it on a patient.' She felt his fingers on her wrist, the thumb pressing firmly between the two bands of muscle that ran down the inside of her arm. 'What do you think?'

'Too many variables. I don't know whether we can come to a definite conclusion.' She was on steadier ground now. Jess ventured a smile.

He chuckled quietly. 'Do you think it matters which arm you do it on?' He'd clearly decided she felt better and had switched to ruminating on variations to his technique.

'I wouldn't know. Here, you want to have a go?' She held out her other arm.

'Hmm. Probably a bit late now.' He grasped her arm anyway and tried again. 'How's that?'

'Feels...okay.' Much, much better than okay. She was starting to tingle all over. Either he'd hit on a discovery that had eluded other medical practitioners for centuries or her body had decided that responding to his touch was a good idea. Great. A little warning might have been in order.

'Jess, we've known each other for long enough...'

'Worked together.' She corrected him quickly. Working together was one kind of knowing. This was another.

'I'm not your boss any more.' Something dark, like liquid promise, glowed in his eyes.

'I suppose that makes things less complicated.'

He grinned. 'Yep. But I won't pretend that I haven't worked alongside you for more hours at a stretch than either of our contracts allows for. I've seen you exhausted, cranky, messy...'

'Thanks a lot!'

'Fabulous, formidable...'

'Better.' They both smiled at the same moment.

'We've got past the point where we need to apologise for all our little foibles.'

'You mean you have foibles?' He did have a way of lifting her worries off her shoulders. Always had.

He shrugged. 'Well, when I said *our foibles* I was just trying to make you feel better about yours.'

'Oh, so you think you don't have foibles?' Jess wrinkled her nose at him. 'What about that famous charm of yours?'

'Doesn't seem to work on you.'

'Works on everyone else.'

'Can I help that?'

'Oh, yeah, you can help it. And the love 'em and leave 'em...'

'It keeps things simple. Anyway, I've changed. The last person I loved and left was...' He frowned, as if consulting his memory and not quite believing the answer he got back.

'Who?'

'You, actually.'

'Me! We didn't....'

He leaned across the table towards her. 'You don't need to. It only takes a touch.' He ran one finger down the back of her hand and Jess gulped, pulling her arm away.

'So what about my foibles, then?' Time to change the subject.

'Your what?' His gaze slid across her body, making her shiver.

'Foibles. Pay attention.'

'I am paying attention.' He pushed the teacups and the plate that stood between them on the table out of the way. 'Okay, so your eyes look as if they have flecks of gold in them. That's not contacts, is it?'

'Of course not.' She nudged her leg against his under the table. 'Foibles, I said.'

'I heard. Well, you're resourceful, talented, generally a force to be reckoned with. Only you don't much like being out of your comfort zone.'

Yes, okay, he might have a point. There were good reasons for her to feel that way. 'Maybe.'

He leaned forward, and Jess couldn't help but move towards him. She felt his lips brush her ear. 'It's a rather nice comfort zone, though.'

'Stop it.' She was feeling better now. As if the weekend wasn't so much of a trial to be got through. Jess almost wished that it was more than two days.

He drew back. From the look in his eyes there was no

question that the dialogue was still continuing somewhere in the back of his mind.

'Do you want to drive?'

'What for?'

'Sometimes driving can help if you're feeling a bit queasy.'

She stared at him. He knew just as well as she did that this was an excuse. That somehow, indefinably, she would feel a bit more in charge of her own destiny if she was in the driving seat. He was good. Good at putting her at her ease. Very, very good at making her want him.

'Okay. If you don't mind.'

He shrugged. 'Why would I mind?'

His car was a pleasure to drive. When she put her foot down on the motorway, it responded with a purr, rather than the laboured growl that her own car would have emitted. Greg pushed the passenger seat back so he could stretch his legs, and confined himself to giving directions. An hour later they turned into a long, gated drive and drew up outside the house.

'It's big.' Jess scanned the complex roof structure, which accommodated an elaborate arrangement of mock crenellations beneath it. There was even a circular tower, tacked onto one side of the building, with a set of battlements and a flagpole at its top.

He grinned. 'Yeah. Not the prettiest of places.'

'It's not meant to be. Victorian, right?'

'Yes, that's right.'

'Then the architecture's not about welcoming visitors, eh?'

He looked again. Leaned back to study the red-brick patterns over the windows and the heavy portico, as if this was the first time he'd seen the place. 'Never really thought about it. So what is it all about, then?'

'It's a statement. This house is all about the people who live here being different from the people who live down in the village. They wanted to impress with their power, not their good taste.'

He nodded. 'You think so?'

Yes, she knew so. The girl from a two-up, two-down felt confronted and challenged by this place and Jess imagined that was exactly how she was meant to feel. 'It's one way of looking at it.'

He nodded, obviously turning the idea over in his head. 'Well, come inside. It's a bit more homely there.'

Not so you'd notice. The large hallway was big enough to contain her whole flat, with height to spare, and the sweeping stone staircase continued the theme of a fortified castle. Leading up to a wide half-landing that was illuminated by a large, stained-glass window, the whole thing reminded her of a film set for a medieval saga.

'Here you are!'

A woman's voice sounded, and for a moment Jess couldn't work out which direction it had come from. Greg turned and made his way towards the back of the hallway.

'We stopped for breakfast.' He spared Jess the indignity of mentioning why. 'What are you doing here?'

A laugh. The first piece of warmth that Jess had met in this place. A figure emerged from the gloom, walking towards her. Mid-fifties, tall and slim. One of those women that made style look like a fortuitous accident.

'I popped in to turn the heating on and put some food in the fridge.' The woman ducked around Greg and made straight for Jess. 'You must be Greg's friend. I'm Rosa.'

'My mother.' Greg was grinning. 'Who never misses a chance to check out who I'm associating with.'

Rosa dismissed him with a casual movement of her fingers. 'Don't be so parochial, darling. Your friends might want to check *me* out.' She grasped Jess's hand, holding it in both of hers, and leaned in to kiss her. 'There. Both cheeks.'

'The Italian way.' Greg was leaning against the heavy stone balustrade which enclosed the stairs, his hands shoved into his pockets.

'Don't listen to my son. I hope you'll come over to my home for something to eat.'

'You live near here?' This was Greg's father's house. He'd said that his mother and father had divorced when he'd been a child, but she seemed very much at home here.

'Two miles in that direction.' Rosa flicked her fingers towards the dark recesses at the back of the hallway. 'You can walk across the fields, it's a nice day.'

Jess shot a questioning look at Greg. Perhaps this wasn't in his plan for the weekend.

'Have you made cannoli?' Greg was smiling at his mother.

'Of course.' Rosa turned to Jess. 'Did he think to tell you to bring any walking shoes?'

No, he hadn't. Jess wasn't sure how well her own shoes would stand up to a cross-country walk. 'Perhaps we can go by road.'

'If you want. Or I think there may be a pair of wellingtons in the cloakroom. If they're too big I'm sure that a couple of pairs of socks...'

'We'll manage.' Greg looked at his watch. 'When do you want us?'

His mother shrugged. 'Whenever you're hungry.'

'How does one o'clock suit you?'

'Perfect. Make it one-ish. Don't worry about being a little late.'

Greg rolled his eyes and kissed his mother, helped her into the waterproof coat that was slung on a low settle in one corner of the hallway and bade her goodbye. Alone again with him, the temperature in the cavernous, empty space seemed to drop a couple of degrees and Jess drew her jacket around her.

'Sorry, Jess. My mother wasn't really checking you out, she's not like that.'

'It was nice of her to come by, this place could do with warming up a bit. I didn't realise that your mother lived so close to your father.'

'My father wasn't here much.' Greg's mouth twitched downwards and he turned away, moving to the door at the back of the hallway where his mother had appeared from. 'He lived mostly in the States, but he came over here three or four times a year to take care of his business interests in Europe.'

'He kept this place empty, then, most of the time?' It was a huge house, even for a family. For one man, who was hardly ever there, it was ridiculous.

'He used to entertain a lot when he was here.' There was a trace of bitterness in Greg's voice.

'I suppose it was handy to see you as well.' Jess followed him into the large, well-equipped kitchen, which could have accommodated an army of caterers.

He raised an eyebrow. 'He was mostly working. Mum used to bring me over, and half the time we'd just make our own entertainment because my father was locked away in the study, on the phone.'

'But she still brought you.' A picture of Rosa, walking her young son across the fields so that he could see his father, floated into her head. How must she have felt when the boy was ignored?

'My mother was an eternal optimist where my father

was concerned. She always encouraged me to see him.'
He dumped the kettle down onto the range and lit the gas
underneath it.

In this house, he seemed surrounded by things he didn't
want to talk about. But he'd come here. He'd brought her
here. On some level he must be aware of that, and that the
seemingly complicated tangle of his relationship with his
father wasn't going to straighten itself out all on its own.

'So this is where you grew up?' She settled herself onto
one of a long row of kitchen stools.

'Yeah.'

'And you didn't see much of your father.'

'Nope. Not a lot.'

She'd hit a sore spot, but she kept pressing. Sometimes
you had to do that. 'But your parents were on good terms?'

He barked out a short laugh. 'Yeah. She loved him, and
in his way he loved her. They just had very different priorities. And it's not particularly easy to maintain a relationship with someone who only has about five uninterrupted
minutes a day to spend with you.'

'No. I imagine not.' Jess wondered whether Greg was
talking about his mother's relationship with his father or
his own. Probably a bit of both. 'Neither of them married
again?'

'Not straight away. But that doesn't mean they were
secretly yearning to get back together. My father had his
share of women friends. They loved the lifestyle for a
while and then realised that they'd always be playing second fiddle to his work. And my mother remarried when
I was fifteen. The local doctor. You'll meet Ted when we
go over there.' There was sudden warmth in his voice.

'So it was his footsteps you followed in.'

'Guess so. Mum made him wait, but he was always there

when I was a kid. He'd take us out somewhere every week-end, we used to have great adventures together.'

'But they never moved away from here?'

'Why should they? Ted's practice is down in the village. This is my mother's home much more than it ever was my father's.' He shrugged. 'Although he came back here at the end.'

'You mean he died here?'

Greg nodded. 'He hadn't told anyone that he had cancer. But when he turned up here, two days after Christmas last year, it was obvious that he was ill. My mother called me, and I arranged for him to be seen by a specialist. My mother looked after him, right up until the end.'

'That was a nice thing to do.'

'Yeah. She's a nice person. I think somehow my father reckoned that he could correct some of the mistakes he'd made, but it was too late.' He poured the tea and set a cup in front of her on the marble worktop. 'Does that cover it?'

'I don't know. Does it?' Greg's secrets ran deeper than this. Nothing that he'd said explained the eight-month absence after his father's death. Or the air of weariness that broke through whenever he talked about his father.

'Difficult to say. Would you like to see the house?'

'Why not?'

CHAPTER FOUR

THE HOUSE WAS full of large, chilly rooms that could have been light if it weren't for the heavy drapes at the windows and the dark wood panelling everywhere. Jess smiled politely and tried to see the best in it all.

'What's through here?' She pointed to the door at the end of the corridor that led from the top of the stairs. If she could find some corner of this house that she could genuinely own up to liking, she was determined to do so.

'It's the inside of the old turret. I used to play in there when I was a kid.' He strode forward, opening the door. 'No one's been in here for a while.'

The room was circular, with tall narrow windows that curved to a point at the top and a complex, many-angled ceiling above their heads. Dust sheets covered what looked like seating and occasional tables.

'This is great, Greg.' This time she could give unqualified praise.

'You like it? It's not very practical.'

'It's fun, though.'

'Yeah, it's definitely fun. I used to fight my way up and down those stairs quite regularly when I was a kid.' He nodded towards the stone stairway, which followed the curve of the wall down to the ground floor.

'Your very own medieval castle.' Complete with a few

ghosts from the past, if the memories flickering in Greg's eyes were anything to go by.

'Yeah.' He was looking around, seeing things she couldn't. 'We had a film crew here once. It was just a B movie and I don't think they set much store by historical accuracy but I loved it. I made my mother bring me here every day, just to watch.' He grinned proudly. 'I had a bit part.'

'Really? Who did you play?'

'A nameless, grubby urchin. Didn't get any lines, but I gave it my all.'

'I'm sure you did. So what's the film?'

'My mother has a copy. I dare say if you ask her, she'll let you savour every moment of my time on the silver screen in glorious slow-mo.' He went to turn but something stopped him. The ghosts weren't done with him yet, and he seemed caught, unable to move, his breath misting white in the chill of the air.

'Those memories are important.'

'They're...' He was making a visible effort to resist some beguiling force, but Jess couldn't tell what, and it was difficult to imagine what Greg could want that he didn't already have. His attention was suddenly focussed back onto her. 'It's cold in here. You're shivering.'

So do something about it. Hold me. Keep me warm. 'I should have packed a warmer sweater.'

'I have a few here.' He turned abruptly. 'Come and pick one out.'

His sweater didn't fit, but it was warm, and Jess could fold the cuffs so that her hands didn't disappear completely. And it smelled of him. Warm and sexy, and not really hers. She'd packed her best jeans, on the off chance she might need them, and Greg produced a pair of wellingtons along with a pair of thick woollen socks from the cloakroom.

'Are you sure it's okay for me to turn up at your mother's looking like this?'

'I think you look rather fetching. Red suits you.' Greg's smile would have made her feel fabulous, even if she'd been wearing rags. 'Anyway, you wouldn't want to make me feel underdressed, would you?'

The idea was faintly ludicrous. His jeans were a shade of something between indigo and black, which you generally didn't find on the high street. His sweater wasn't new, but it was soft, thick cashmere, like the one he'd lent her. Coupled with those dark good looks, he was quality from head to toe and would have fitted in anywhere.

He caught his car keys up from the hall table. 'I'll get your coat from the car.'

They tramped across the fields, keeping up a brisk pace against the cold. Jess was glad of the woollen scarf and gloves that Greg had produced from the cloakroom, which was beginning to take on the nature of a magician's cubby hole, from which it was possible to conjure up all manner of useful things that appeared to belong to no one in particular.

'That's where we're headed.' He pointed towards a house, standing on the outskirts of the village.

'It looks lovely.' Jess didn't have to search for something nice to say this time. The yellow-brick, rambling farmhouse was everything that Greg's father's house wasn't. Blending in with the trees and evergreen bushes that surrounded it, as if it had just grown there instead of having been brutally hewn from the countryside. 'This was your real home, then.'

'Yeah.' His pace seemed to quicken, the nearer they

got. As if he was leaving some burden behind. 'Where did you grow up?'

Jess smiled. 'Nowhere so grand.'

He twisted the corners of his mouth down. 'This isn't so very grand, is it?'

'It is quite grand. We didn't have our own medieval tower at home.'

'It's only mock-medieval—' He broke off, grinning. 'Yeah, I suppose the tower's not your average home extension. But stop changing the subject. I've already spilled the beans.'

Maybe he had. Maybe he'd just told her what he wanted her to know and kept the rest back. 'Not much to know. Just me and my mum. We had a little house in South London.'

He nodded. 'No brothers or sisters?'

'No. My father left before I was born.' Jess shrugged. 'I don't miss him. I can't, I didn't know him.'

'Can't you miss things that you didn't have?'

'I'm not sure there were any.' She answered too quickly. Maybe even a bit defensively.

He laughed. 'May I have your autograph?'

'Why?'

'I've never met anyone who's had everything they ever wanted before.'

Jess nudged her shoulder against his arm. 'Don't be dense, Greg. There's not much point in wanting things you're never going to have.'

'No. But sometimes you have to acknowledge them.'

'Because?'

'Because you can't start to work on what you need, unless you acknowledge what's missing.'

Maybe. She'd need to think about that. 'I guess I miss knowing about him. Silly things, like whether my eyes are the same colour as his. Whether there's anything in his medical history that I should be watching out for.'

He chuckled. 'Always good to know. Have you any idea where he is now?'

'In a manner of speaking. He was killed in a car accident fifteen years ago. Someone came to tell Mum.' Jess remembered that day well enough. The stranger who'd knocked on their door, and who her mother had taken into the kitchen to talk with privately. The silence in the house, and then the sudden resumption of normal life, as if her mother had made a conscious decision to put all of that behind her and never speak of it again.

Greg's pace slowed and he found her hand, tucking it under his arm. They fell into step together almost automatically. 'Did anyone ever say they were sorry? For that loss?'

'No. No one ever thought it was one.' It was what Jess had told herself, too.

'I'm sorry. For your loss.'

'Thank you.' She smiled up at him. He must have repeated that phrase any number of times in his career, but he always seemed to mean it. It came as a surprise to find how much it meant to her, too.

'Can I ask you a question, Greg?'

'Since when did you need permission for that?'

'How did you feel when your mother remarried? I mean…did you mind?'

'Mind? Well, Ted was practically living with us anyway. And we all went to Italy and had an enormous party, and I got to stay with my aunt, while they went off on honeymoon. I kissed a girl, broke my arm coming off my cousin's motorbike and generally had a whale of a time. My mother was horrified when she got back.'

'I bet she was. How old did you say you were?'

'Fifteen.'

'Hmm. My mother married when I was twenty.'

'And?'

'And her husband's a really nice man. He gives her the life she's always deserved and she's happy with him.'

'That's nice. And?'

He waited. Laid his gloved hand over hers, tucking it more firmly into the crook of his arm.

'I don't know if I should even say it. It sounds so stupid…'

'Oh, go on.' He chuckled. 'You can't leave me hanging now.'

Why not? He'd done the same to her. But if Jess gave a little, maybe he would. 'It was just a bit confusing. All my life she'd been telling me that we could manage on our own, that I didn't need a father and she didn't need a husband. Then all of a sudden she upped and got married.'

He chuckled. 'Must have been love.'

'Yeah. Suppose it must have been.' Jess wrinkled her nose.

'Did you look that disapproving when she broke the news?'

'No! Of course I didn't. I'm happy for her, of course I am. I just… When I was little I used to think that it would be me who would get a great job, find somewhere nice for us to live. That I'd be the one to make sure she was comfortable.' Jess forced a smile. 'I'm just being silly.'

He shrugged. 'Sounds reasonable enough to me. You know the trouble with people—families in particular, I've noticed—is that you have these great plans for them, how you're going to make everything right and so on, and then they just go out and do it all on their own. It's frustrating.'

Jess couldn't help laughing now. 'Is that a touch of megalomania I hear?'

'More than a touch, I imagine. Aren't all kids megalomaniacs? That's what growing up does to you, makes you realise that you can't control the world.'

'Oh, so you're saying that I need to grow up, are you?' Jess suspected that she probably did.

'Don't you dare. Stay as you are.' He grinned at her and quickened his pace. 'Only perhaps you could walk just a bit faster. We'll be late if we don't hurry.'

Being late didn't seem to figure much in Rosa's household. Dinner was cooking on the range, and Greg and Jess were both kissed and seated in the warm, bright kitchen. Ted arrived, kicking the mud from his boots at the back door, and Greg rose to meet him, their handshake giving way to a hug.

'I hear you're a doctor.' He accepted a glass of wine from his wife and sat down, next to Jess.

'Yes. I've been specialising in cardiology for the last year.'

Ted nodded. 'Interesting. I expect you're at the sharp end of things, working down in London.'

'The department's done some groundbreaking work in the last couple of years. I'm very junior, though.' Jess grinned. 'But I get to watch sometimes.'

Ted laughed. 'Best way to learn.'

'She's being modest,' Greg broke in. 'She's a rising star in the department.'

'A young woman with a bright future, then.' Ted was watching her thoughtfully and Jess felt herself flush.

The meal was served and eaten and Jess was forbidden from moving when it came to clearing the plates away. Rosa and Greg busied themselves with the washing up, leaving Jess to talk to Ted. 'Your practice must serve quite a big area. In comparison to London.'

'Yes. There are three of us, and we cover about sixty square miles. We keep busy.'

'It must be demanding. Not many of you to go around.'

'It has its moments.' Ted reached for the pot to pour himself a second cup of coffee, and the sharp note of a phone sounded.

'Oh!' Rosa made a splash in the washing-up water with her hand. 'Really?'

Ted smiled. 'Looks like it.' He reached for the phone.

'What?' Everyone but Jess seemed to know what the call was about before Ted had even answered the phone.

'Ted's an immediate care doctor. Means he's on call for any emergencies where ambulance personnel need support at the scene. That's his alert phone.' Greg had put the dish-cloth down and was waiting, watching Ted.

'Okay. Yes, tell them I've accepted the call.' Ted snapped the phone shut and looked at Greg. 'There's a pile-up on the motorway. Want to take a ride with me?'

Greg was already reaching for his jacket and grinned towards Jess. 'Are you coming?'

'If that's all right?' She shot a querying look at Ted.

'I never turn down a helping hand.' Ted turned to Rosa. 'Sorry, darling.'

'Go.' Rosa was clearly used to this kind of thing. 'Just come back again.'

Ted chuckled. If Rosa's return smile was anything to go by, they'd worked this one out a long time ago.

It was beginning to get dark, shadows reaching across the lanes in front of them, as if to smother what was left of the day. Ted joined the motorway and hit the siren, speeding towards the site of the accident.

'There, look.' Greg indicated a slew of stationary head-lights up ahead.

'I see it.' Ted guided the SUV into a space and got out.

Jess could see flashing blue lights approaching from the other direction, and hoped that it was an ambulance.

They moved as if choreographed. Ted was in the lead, the reflective panels on his jacket advertising his presence. Greg was half a step behind him, medical bag and torch in hand, stopping to listen to a man who had detached himself from the small crowd that had gathered around three vehicles, which the force of impact had locked together, like in some gruesome sci-fi movie.

'Okay, take me to her.' Greg turned, beckoning to Jess to follow him, and the man led them to an upturned car.

'She's under there.' Panic was welling in the man's voice as he pointed to the tangled wreckage. 'We couldn't get her out. It's her leg, it's trapped.'

'That's okay. We'll take care of her.' Greg stripped off his jacket and dropped it on the ground. 'Jess, will you see what other casualties we have?'

He didn't look around to catch her assent. He didn't need to. Jess jogged over towards Ted, pushing through the circle of people that surrounded him.

'What have you got?'

'Someone's trapped underneath a car there. Greg's going to see if he can reach her.'

'Okay. I've a couple here, but there's nothing major. You go and assist Greg.' Ted passed her his car keys. 'Take the green bag from the car over to him.'

'Thanks.' Jess took the keys and made for the car, pulling out the large holdall in the back, hoping it would contain whatever they needed. She could see Greg carefully manoeuvring himself under the wreckage, trying to reach the injured woman, and doubted that her leg was his immediate concern. He couldn't treat her here. All he needed to do was to keep her alive until she got to the hospital.

She jogged over to the car, dumping the bag on the

ground and calling out to Greg to let him know she was there. A slight nod of his head told her that he'd heard, and that was all he needed to know for the time being. She could see the woman now, her leg pinned under the collapsed steering column, apparently unconscious.

The side of a truck blocked the driver's door and Greg had crawled in via the passenger door, twisting his body around the buckled frame to examine the woman as best he could in the cramped space. Jess unzipped the bag and quickly looked through the contents, arranging what she might need to one side.

They worked as if they were one unit. They'd done this before, although not for a while now, but the passage of time hadn't dulled their edge. Greg worked quickly, Jess putting what he needed into his hand, almost before he had a chance to ask for it.

'I think she's waking up.' Jess saw the fingers of the woman's outstretched hand flutter then clench. 'Pain relief?' Jess got the words out two seconds before the woman started to scream.

'Yep.' Greg's head snapped back as a flailing hand caught him square in the face, and he struggled for a moment to control his patient. 'Okay. Okay. I'm a doctor. You're going to be okay. We're getting you something for the pain.' He held her tight. Not just to stop her from moving and injuring herself any further, but for comfort. The screams subsided and the woman whimpered in his arms.

He called out the dosage, and Jess slid carefully inside the car, gasping as the sharp smell of blood and sheared metal hit her. She could reach the woman's arm, and she cut the sleeve of her coat and searched for a vein. 'Okay... That's it...done.'

'Good. Now go.' His voice was suddenly harsh, an order

instead of a request, and Jess wriggled backwards out of the wreckage.

She wished he wouldn't do that. He was the senior doctor, and there was no need for two of them to run the risk of being inside the wreckage. All the same, it rankled somehow that she wasn't by his side. The firefighters had just arrived on the scene, and she was pushed aside so that the senior man could speak directly to Greg and assess the situation.

She heard Ted's voice behind her. 'The hardest decision is knowing when to step back.'

Jess composed her face into a smile and turned. 'I just do as I'm told.'

'Really?' A smile played around Ted's lips. 'I'd be disappointed if that turned out to be true.'

He pulled her to one side, as someone came through with props to shore up the unstable wreckage. She could hardly see Greg now, masked by twisted metal and concentrated activity.

Ted was still watching every move that the firefighters made. 'See, they're going to cut through there. It won't be long now, and Greg knows what he's doing.'

'Yes, he does. He's a great doctor.'

Ted nodded, with the air of a suspicion confirmed. 'Damn shame.'

'What?'

'If he decided to re-evaluate his priorities.'

'But he's only just back from…' Jess stared at Ted. His measured demeanour wasn't just for show, he'd said no more and no less than intended. What *was* going on with Greg?

She could find that out later. For now it was enough to watch as the fire crew began the task of carefully peeling back the layers of metal that imprisoned the woman. She had calmed as the morphine kicked in, and Jess could hear Greg talking to her in between the shouts and the sounds of machinery. She knew he'd be watching her like a hawk, checking her responses, her BP, her pulse. His job was to make sure that she was brought out of the wreckage alive, and his quiet, reassuring tones were all part of the fight that he was putting up to do so.

Greg had shielded her face with his hand, holding her as the final agonising manoeuvres removed the metal that was trapping her legs. And then, at last, she was out.

CHAPTER FIVE

TINA WAS FREE of the twisted wreckage. Her leg was badly broken and she had a few nasty cuts, but she was comfortable and on her way to hospital. Greg smiled to himself as he watched the blue lights disappearing over the brow of a hill. He couldn't ignore the buzz. The excitement of meeting a challenge. The feeling that he'd helped make the biggest difference of all to someone.

It was starting to sleet, and when he turned, Jess was standing behind him. Little shards of ice were beginning to stick to her hair, and one glistened on her eyelashes. The temptation to brush it away hit him hard and twisted remorselessly in his chest.

'Good job.'

She was smiling at him. Greg wondered whether it was her smile or her words that meant the most to him. Perhaps they were inseparable.

'This is what you were meant to do, Greg.'

He didn't want to get into that at the moment. He was tired and Jess was beginning to shiver. 'Is Ted ready to go?'

'Yes, he's in the car.' She gestured towards the SUV.

'Let's make tracks, then.'

Greg stayed long enough to see Ted tip himself into an armchair and then borrowed his mother's car keys to take

Jess home. She was wet, cold and dirty. Lovely beyond any accepted sense of the word.

'I think I need a shower.' She grinned at him, half-apologetically.

'Yeah. Me too.' Greg saw her flush slightly and elaborated quickly. 'Your room has an en suite bathroom.' Therefore his did too. Two geographically separate showers. 'I'll get the fire going in the living room and heat up some soup.'

'Sounds fabulous.' She gave him a smile and made for the stairs.

The house didn't do sunny at all. It didn't really do welcoming, and Greg was aware that although he'd stopped noticing that a long time ago, Jess hadn't failed to. What it did do tolerably well was long winter evenings, curled up in front of the fire. Greg lit the firelighters in the grate, and arranged a couple of easy chairs close enough to catch the heat when the blaze got going.

She took her time upstairs. Greg had showered, heated the soup and bought a tray through to the living room before some sixth sense alerted him of her presence behind him.

'What have you been doing up there?' He turned and almost dropped the mug of soup that he was holding. She looked like cotton candy. Pink cheeks and a thick, white towelling robe that she'd found in the bathroom, with pink pyjamas on underneath. Thick socks on her feet. Wet hair, combed back from her face. Greg nearly choked with desire.

'Is it okay to use this?' She tugged at the robe.

'Of course. That's what they're there for.' He didn't even know were they came from. They were just there, and the housekeeper who came in three times a week made sure that they were laundered and fresh in all the guest rooms. 'Come and sit down.'

'Thanks.' She sat, tucking her legs up beneath her. Greg handed her a mug of soup and she rewarded him with a smile of complete happiness.

He stoked the fire until flames began to crackle in the grate. Sat back down in his chair and allowed himself to watch her. Relaxed, curled up in an armchair, revelling in the heat of the fire.

'Can I ask you a question?' Her gaze was steady on his face and Greg almost flinched.

'Of course.'

'What did you feel? When you got that woman out of the car.'

That sounded like a trick question. 'You know what I felt.'

'Yes, I do. I just wanted to make sure that...' She paused, studying the flames. 'That you hadn't lost that feeling. Or reconsidered it. Anything like that.'

What had Ted been saying to her? Or perhaps his mother had dragged her off into a corner somewhere for one of those woman-to-woman chats. But Ted and his mother knew no more than Jess did. Perhaps he was just not as good at hiding it as he'd thought.

'It doesn't get old. You saw Ted, he's been a doctor for thirty years and he still gets a thrill out of what he does.'

'Good. That's good.' She was watching the fire as if it contained the answer to everything. As if she could see her dreams reflected in it, if she only looked hard enough. 'When you were away...'

'Not tonight, Jess. Please.'

'You don't know what I was about to say.'

'Whatever it is.' He leaned back in his chair, letting the warmth from the fire relax his knotted muscles. Just one evening off from the continual, nagging demands that had dogged him from one side of the Atlantic to the other. 'Can we talk about it another time?'

She didn't seem sorry to let it go for a while, shifting in her chair, snuggling and stretching like a cat. 'Okay. Another time.'

He put some music on. Sleepy background music, playing softly so that it didn't drown out their conversation. The talk drifted, sliding effortlessly from the plans for Christmas at the hospital to model making and then on to storytelling.

'This is just the place. An open fire, cold outside, not another soul for miles.' She grinned wickedly. 'It was a dark and stormy night...'

'And the electricity was off.'

'And the water.'

'Water? Does that matter?' She shrugged and he grinned at her. 'Okay, then the gas is off too.'

She snorted with laughter. 'That doesn't matter either. Ghosts don't mind gas.'

'How do you know?'

'They're ephemeral beings. They are probably some sort of gas themselves.'

'If you say so. The gas was on, then, and the candle-light flickered low around the people stranded in the middle of nowhere.'

'Whose car had broken down.'

'And then they realised that they'd both forgotten to re-charge their phones.'

'Yep. And the landline's down as well.'

'And the walk down to the next village is blocked by snow.'

'And they've forgotten their snow boots.' She was laughing now.

'Reasonable enough thing to do. So they're alone in the house, quite unaware that something's lurking.'

'And they put some music on…'

'I thought the electricity was out.'

She grinned. 'He's very resourceful, he's managed to fix it. They put some music on to drown out the sound of the rain on the windows and the bumps and creaks in the house.'

'Yeah. Only it's snowing, not raining.'

'Snow doesn't make a noise on the windows.'

'Sleet, then.'

'Okay, sleet.' She nodded, the way she always did when she considered something sorted. In the firelight she was almost unbearably beautiful. 'They turn the music up loud, because they're out in the country now and don't have to worry about disturbing the neighbours.'

'Like this.' Greg leaned over, sweeping his finger across the shiny surface of his mp3 player, choosing a slow dance track and cranking up the volume.

'Just like that.' Her fingers started to follow the beat, moving gently on the arm of her chair. Almost a caress.

'And they dance.' The story was taking a volatile turn, but Greg didn't care. It was just a story. Something to ward off the darkness.

She hesitated. 'She's not really dressed for dancing.'

'But it doesn't matter, because she's exquisitely beautiful in the firelight.' Greg got to his feet. Took her hand and in response to his gentle tug she was on her feet. In his arms.

It was just the way it had been before. Jess could ward off all manner of bad spirits and all of his fears for the future. There was no past, no future, just the present. He led their slow dance, circling her in front of the fire.

'Nice.' The music has finished but they were still dancing, bodies pressed together. No friction, just moving in perfect synchronisation. 'This is nice, Greg.'

'Just nice?'

'Lovely.' She rested her head on his chest and he caught the clean scent of her hair. 'Scary.'

'Stick with me. You said I was very resourceful.'

She laughed quietly, snuggling closer to him. She wanted this as much as he did. A break from reality, where they could just follow their own instincts. Right now his instinct was to kiss her.

She didn't stop him. Let him press his lips against her cheek, taste the warmth of her skin. When he ran one thumb over her lips, she shivered slightly against him. And when he kissed her mouth she gave a sigh, as if she'd been holding her breath, waiting for this.

'What are we doing, Greg?'

'Dancing.' He brushed his lips against her cheek. 'Kissing.'

'Is it a good idea?'

'Yeah. It's a very good idea. Last Christmas...it wasn't just a mistake that's better off forgotten.'

'It was a long time ago.'

'It was just yesterday. Nothing's changed.' Everything had changed, but Greg could find his way back. Pretend that tonight was a loop in time, and they could simply pick up where they'd left off.

'You sure about that?'

'I'm not very sure about a lot of things at the moment.' He took her hand and laid it over his heart. 'This, I'm sure of.'

'Yeah.' She managed a watery smile. 'Tachycardia. You might think about making an appointment with Gerry.'

'I'd rather you dealt with it.' He laid his hand over hers,

sliding it inside his shirt, feeling his skin react to the heat of her touch. Electricity buzzed in the air around them.

Her hands slid to his neck and then up, to cup his face. 'Does this mean…?' She shrugged. 'I don't even know what it means.'

He laid a finger to her lips. 'It means just you and me, for tonight. Every moment until the sun rises. Everything else will wait.'

'Yes. I think it will.' She pulled his head down towards her, and kissed him. Drew back slightly, confident that if she gave him one taste, he'd take a second.

One hand moved to the tie of her bathrobe and he caught her wrist. 'I'll do it.' He'd fantasised about undressing her for too many months to miss it now.

'Hmm. Not exactly silk and lace.'

He laughed against her lips. 'Warmer. Nicer.'

'You're such a charmer, Greg.' That friendly, one-quarter mocking tone that she used whenever he tried to dress things up with pretty words. Jess was about the only woman he knew who talked about his charm, the rest of them just lapped it up and fell victim to it.

'So it's not working?'

'It's working.' She planted a kiss on his lips and charm suddenly felt as if it was a private joke, just between the two of them. Something that made her smile but didn't touch the honest, down-to-earth fire that he wanted more than anything else that he could think of.

Actions now. He was trembling like a teenager, afraid of not doing this right. It was crazy. He knew how to please a woman. But, then, Jess wasn't just any woman.

Carefully, he tugged at the knot at her waist, fumbling with it. It came loose and he slipped the bathrobe down her shoulders, tightening his grip when it reached her elbows and pulling her against him. She gasped with delight.

'Do you think I'm going to put up a struggle?'

He almost let go, shocked at the strength of his urgency, and then she kissed him again. Arms pinioned at her sides, almost helpless, and loving every moment of his desire for her.

'Are you going to, then?'

'Oh, yeah. Every time.' She slipped free of the bathrobe and it fell at her feet. 'You?'

'I think I might.' He'd lose. Greg knew that he couldn't resist her and that he couldn't protect himself with well-worn phrases or practised caresses. This was uncharted territory, and, dammit, it he just couldn't keep himself away from it.

He unbuttoned her pyjama top, finding that there was another layer underneath. Good. A pretty, lace trimmed vest, which somehow managed to combine the practical with the erotic.

'My turn.' She undid the buttons of his shirt, her tongue pressed between her lips in concentration. Pulled it away from his shoulders and tossed it away. The soft pressure of her fingers on his shoulders overwhelmed him, and Greg fell to one knee on the hearthrug in front of her.

'Now you.' His hands on her hips held her steady, and he nodded towards the vest.

'Don't you want to do it?'

'I want to watch.'

She pulled it off, shaking her head slightly to free herself. Breathing fast, but steadily, as if she was trying to pace herself. His hands put an end to that and she gasped then cried out.

He explored the smooth skin of her arms, the lush curves of her breasts. Ran his finger down her spine, to the sensitive knot of nerves in the small of her back, and she shivered, sagging forward against his shoulder. Greg pulled at the waistband of her pyjama bottoms, and slid them down, pulling her socks off, one by one, in a slow, tender striptease.

She pulled him to his feet, her gaze fixed on his face. Greg felt her fingers on his belt buckle, gently working it loose. Held in the luminous fire of her gaze, he felt rather than saw her undo the top button on his jeans.

'Sit down.' Greg let her back him towards an armchair, and almost collapsed into it. He wanted this. Wanted to offer his body to her in all its frailty, and let her break him and put him back together again.

She was down on her knees, completely naked, unlacing his shoes. Carefully slipping them off, as firelight flickered across her skin, bathing it in warmth and texture. He'd never seen anything so beautiful before in his life.

'Jess.' He leaned forward to kiss her. The time was right. Pulling the heavy throw from the sofa onto the floor in front of the fire, he laid her down on it. She was pulling at the fastenings of his jeans now, and he batted her hands away. 'Not yet, honey. This is all for you.'

Who wouldn't be beguiled by those words? Before he lifted her up, carrying her swiftly up the wide staircase, he'd already made good on their promise, right there in the flickering shadows of the hearth. Caresses that had made every part of her body react.

Soft, whispered words, kisses that had made her shiver in the heat of anticipation. When his slow, steady assault on her senses had proved too much, tearing the last of her inhibitions away, he'd held her tight in his arms, as if he'd known that she'd needed some protection from the fierce power of her own desire for him.

His bedroom was in darkness, and she wasn't there to admire the furniture anyway. The sudden chill of the sheets when he laid her down was just another sensation, another pleasure to nerve endings that were fast becoming unable to register anything else.

'Greg. I need...'

'I know what you need.' It wasn't just a hollow piece of male swagger. He did know what she needed. And somehow she knew just what he needed, too.

'Some light.' Before she'd said it, he had already been reaching for the switch by the bed, and a couple of lamps glowed into life.

'It's cold in here.' He curled his body around hers, wrapping her in his warmth.

'I need to breathe.' Her need for him was so urgent that she'd almost forgotten how.

He settled her beneath him, holding her tight. In one slow, smooth movement he was inside her, and Jess cried out. Sucked in a lungful of air and gasped it back out again as he moved.

'I need you to do that again.'

Greg had slept for a just a few blissful, unbroken hours before he woke, but it felt like more. Quietly, carefully, so as not to disturb Jess, he got out of bed and slipped on his jeans and a sweater.

As he passed through the hallway, the clock downstairs chimed midnight. Jess had just shaken his world, along with rocking, rolling and turning it upside down. Greg made for the one place in this house where he'd always been able to be alone and to think clearly.

This Christmas...

He was in love. The realisation hit Greg like a hammer, almost flattening him. But as he drifted gently forward in time, a week, then two, he rather got to like the idea. When Christmas came, his one thought was how he could make it special for Jess.

Did his father's company have a private jet at its disposal? Greg was sure that it probably did. He could take Jess somewhere sunny for Christmas, an island that was secluded enough for them to make love on the beach, without any fear of being discovered.

Greg reconsidered for a moment. Was that really so practical? Maybe not up till now but, then, he'd never had Pat's unending resourcefulness at his disposal. If anyone could locate a deserted tropical island for Christmas, Pat could.

For the purposes of reorientation he ran through the part about making love on the beach again. Then once more, with a set of subtle but enormously rewarding amendments. He could almost taste the salt on her warm skin.

He could afford to give Jess everything. She didn't need to work, she could do whatever she pleased. She could travel with him, and a little charity work would appease her need to help others.

Was he serious? The thought of Jess giving up her career in favour of sipping cocktails and doing a little charity work was about as likely as... Well, it was impossible. There had to be something else.

There was something else. He would have to dump the company he'd inherited from his father and had been struggling to save for the last eight months, but it was surprising how good the prospect felt. That would leave him with nothing to worry about other than how tall a Christmas tree the ceilings of his apartment would allow, and nowhere else to spend his time other than with Jess. Presents in the morning, a visit to the hospital to see how the

*carol singers were doing, and then on to his mother's for
one of those late lunches that she did with such aplomb.*

He'd so hoped...

*Greg put up a struggle before he reluctantly let go of
the fantasy and it disappeared back into his subconscious.
This wasn't the time for hopes. Dreams either, although
if this wasn't one then Greg wasn't sure what he should
call it. Did he really think that he was going to be able
to watch Shaw Industries go down, just because he had
somewhere else to be? Would Jess ever respect him for
abandoning the people who had worked for his father and
now worked for him? People who had families to support,
workers who were close to retirement and would struggle
to find another job.*

*He had to face facts. His father, the ultimate autocrat,
had structured the company to fail without him, or his son,
to provide strong leadership. Like it or not, he was the only
one left now. He was going to have to find a way to balance it all, something for the company, something for Jess,
and whatever was left over for himself. He couldn't think
about the chances against that working. All he could do
was make a lunge for the slim thread of hope that it might.*

CHAPTER SIX

JESS WOKE UP alone. The clock registered ten minutes past midnight, and she stretched her limbs and turned over to go back to sleep.

When had that happened? This inability to sleep without Greg beside her? She turned over again, burrowing deep into the duvet, and then gave up.

He wasn't downstairs in the living room, and Jess skittered over to the fireside, still warm from the glowing embers in the grate. Pulling on her dressing gown and socks, which still lay discarded on the floor, she made for the kitchen.

Not there either. It was as if Greg had vanished completely, sucked back into the vortex of the real world. She wasn't quite ready for that. Just a little more time in this no-man's land, where the unthinkable might just come true.

She padded back upstairs, wondering whether she should put her head around all the bedroom doors. Then a line of light under the door at the end of the corridor, which led to the tower room, changed her mind.

The grandfather clock in the hallway started to go through the truncated chimes that heralded the quarter-hour. Jess twisted the handle of the door, opening it quietly. Greg hadn't bothered to strip the dust sheet off the chair, and sat on it with his back to her, seemingly staring out of the window at the moon as it hung silently in the sky.

'Greg?' Her breath streamed white in the cold air. 'It's freezing in here.'

If she'd crashed two trays together next to his head, he probably wouldn't have jumped any further. He twisted round, a look of blank shock on his face.

'What's the matter? You look as if you've seen a ghost.' Jess regretted the words immediately. You generally said that kind of thing to people who clearly hadn't seen a ghost. For one moment she wasn't quite sure whether she hadn't hit the nail squarely on the head.

He recovered himself, reaching for her, and she let him pull her down onto his lap. 'You feel solid enough.'

'You're checking?'

'Best to be sure.' He kissed her, taking his time, and something stirred inside her. Something that had already had its fill and ought to be fast asleep now.

'What are you doing in here?'

He shrugged. 'I couldn't sleep, so I thought I'd get up for half an hour, rather than disturb you. I must have dozed off.'

'I woke up and you weren't there.'

His lip curled slightly, in obvious gratification. 'Couldn't sleep without me?'

'You think it's a good thing that you have a soporific effect on me?'

His eyes taunted her. 'You think there was any danger of you going to sleep one minute before I let you?'

She planted a kiss on the end of her finger and transferred it to his forehead. 'In other words, I'm like putty in your hands?'

He slipped his hand inside her gown, trailing his cool

fingers across the warm skin of her leg, and she shivered with delight. 'Looks as if you are.'

'Come back to bed.'

He grinned. 'Yes, ma'am. Whatever you say.'

As soon as he had her back in his bedroom he stripped her naked, his own clothes slung on top of hers on the armchair in the corner of the room. The bed was still warm, and Jess curled up beside him.

'Mmm. That's better.'

'Much.' His hand wandered across her ribcage. 'Jess, what are you doing for Christmas?'

She smiled into his shoulder. Christmas with Greg would be wonderful. 'I'm staying in London. There's a lot to do at the hospital.'

'Won't that all be organised by then? You deserve some time off.'

'I'll have time off. But I can't ask people to give up their time over Christmas without being there myself.' That didn't seem to be what Greg wanted to hear. 'Why?'

'Nothing. I just wondered.' He rolled her over onto her back, kissing her, lingering over her lips until he'd taken his fill. 'Maybe I can persuade you differently.'

'Not like that, you can't.'

'Oh, really? Is that a challenge?'

'No. Would you want to be able to change my mind when you know I'm doing something worthwhile?'

He didn't answer. The Greg she knew wouldn't have had to. As she gave herself up to his caress, the final, fleeting thought in Jess's head was that she hoped this was the Greg that she was sleeping with.

It was barely light when she opened her eyes. She was warm, almost blissfully relaxed, and alone again.

Where was Greg now? She clambered out of bed and

opened the door, craning her head around it, half expecting to see the door at the end of the hallway open.

Greg's voice sounded, quiet and muffled from downstairs. A pause, and then he spoke again. He was talking to someone.

She felt like a spy. As if she was snooping around his house, trying to catch him doing something he clearly didn't want her to know about. But he'd deflected the conversation too many times, left too much unanswered. He was hiding something. Jess moved noiselessly along the hallway, pausing at the top of the great stairway and leaning over the stone balustrade.

'The new controls do involve extra work, though, Ed. Everyone deserves to be paid for the hours they put in.'

Another pause.

'Ed, that's the end of it. I've reviewed all the options, and that's the fairest for everyone... No, that's final.' Greg's voice was firm, decisive. No surprise there. But the note of irritable bad temper didn't sound like him. Jess tried to turn away but she couldn't and instead she sank to the floor, as if the rough, stone buttresses could shield her from what she was hearing.

'No, I realise that, Ed. I'll prepare something for the board, so that they all know exactly where this directive is coming from. When's the meeting? Ten on Tuesday. That's nine o' clock Monday night our time, isn't it? Right. I'll get back to you before then.'

Eleven hours' time difference. That was the other side of the world. America was eight hours at most, wasn't it? And yet this sounded like business talk, certainly nothing to do with the hospital. Jess heard a clatter as a telephone handset was put back into its cradle and she sprang to her feet, racing up the hallway towards the guest room where her overnight bag still sat on the undisturbed bed. In less than a minute she was in the shower, the door firmly locked behind her.

So what on earth was he supposed to do? Greg took his feelings out on the loaf of bread that he was cutting for toast, and had to throw the resulting slice into the bin. He had a chance to make a difference here. The hours weren't exactly regular, but neither were they at the hospital. He had hoped that Jess might understand.

He'd been aware that she was there, even before he'd put the phone down, and had heard her blundering along the hallway. Greg couldn't deny that his exaggerated sense of his own innocence had something to do with the fact that he also felt guilty as hell.

There was only so long that he could resent Jess, though. And with the scent of her still on his skin, the feel of her echoing through his memory, *only so long* wasn't very long at all. She walked into the kitchen, showered and dressed, and Greg was lost again.

'Hey, there. You're up early.' He bent to kiss her but the immediate fit that had moulded them together last night was lost now, and his lips brushed her cheek instead of her mouth.

'So are you. I woke up and you weren't there.'

'I had something to do.'

Her look, half hurt and half suspicious, made his mind up for him. He could break his rule, just once. He'd let her ask him about the business and then she wouldn't need to wonder again.

He waited until she had coffee and toast in front of her, and sat down next to her at the breakfast bar. 'There's something I want to talk to you about.'

She turned her gaze on him, thoughtful and shot through

with golden tenderness. She'd done that last night, when the honesty had got too much to bear, soothing him, letting him know that it was all right.

'I wanted to talk to you about what I've been doing for the last eight months.'

She couldn't disguise her reaction and she didn't try. 'I have been wondering. I'm glad you want to talk about it.'

'You might like to wait until you've heard what it is.'

'Whatever it is, it can hardly be as fantastical as the hospital gossip.'

'There was gossip?' Of course there had been gossip. It was one of the oddities of life that in an institution devoted to the sick, you only had to sneeze and someone remarked on it.

She smiled. 'What do you think? Opinion was split between you having a secret twin that you'd gone to find and you having inherited countless millions. There was some talk of a treasure map, but that one didn't run for too long. I think Gerry suggested it as a polite way of shutting everyone up and it backfired on him.'

'No one said anything.'

'Everyone's forgotten about it now.' She smiled at him. 'I'm afraid you only get fifteen minutes of fame. Then no one remembers your name.'

He laughed. She made everything so easy. That was part of what had made her such an invaluable part of his team. No expectations, no prejudices. Just find out what the situation is and deal with it.

'So what was it really, then?' She was gently prodding him in the right direction.

'Well, there's no lost twin. No treasure map.' He almost regretted the absence of both. In fact, a treasure map might have been an adventure. 'The countless millions are a bit closer to the mark, although I believe my accountant knows how many there are.'

She was frowning. 'But, it's obvious that your father was wealthy—this is a big house. Is there a problem with that?'

'No, Jess.' She wasn't understanding him. 'My father was a *very* rich man.' He put as much emphasis as he could on the 'very'. 'Houses on three continents. A multi-million-pound business that I'm only just coming to grips with how to run. A racehorse.'

'A racehorse!' This was all taking time to sink in, and the rest was beyond her grasp at the moment. 'What's its name?'

'I have no idea. I don't really want to know, I might start getting attached to it.'

'Three continents?' She was getting there.

'Yeah. One in Australia, two in America, one in Rome and one here. The one in Rome's really nice.'

She was shrinking back from him, as if he'd just admitted to being an imposter from outer space who'd taken over his own body.

'I could take you there for a holiday, over Christmas maybe. I think you'd love it.'

She swallowed hard. 'But it's the business, isn't it? That's what the problem is.'

She might be feeling acutely flabbergasted, but you could never accuse Jess of not being able to size up a situation.

'Yes, exactly. My father and I weren't particularly close and he wasn't best pleased when I decided to go to medical school. It would have been nice to have a few personal things of his, but I'd always counted on him leaving his business interests to someone involved with the business.'

'But you're his son!' It made Greg smile to hear her assert his filial rights. 'You're his only child?'

He nodded. 'Yeah, no long-lost siblings. Or if there are, they're keeping quiet and I can't say I blame them. It's down to me to sort everything out.'

Jess stared at him. Most people would have been over-joyed to hear of such an inheritance. Most women would already be planning the trip to Rome. Somehow she didn't seem to be quite on board with that. 'But isn't that what you were doing when you were away?'

'I've made a start.' He took a sip of his espresso. 'The board of directors is split over practically every issue you can name. My father chose people who were ambitious and who would think out of the box. He was the ultimate authority who kept it all under control, and that worked well when he was alive. Now it's tearing itself apart at the seams.'

'And...you mean you're still running it?'

'Not the day-to-day stuff. But, yes, I'm running it. I don't have much choice; there are thousands of people de-pending on it for their livelihoods.'

'Couldn't you sell it?'

'Yes. But it needs to be sold as a going concern.' In truth, Greg hadn't even considered selling up. 'And it was so important to my father...'

'That's the thing, isn't it? It was the most important thing in his life and now he's given it to you. And if you give it up, it's like having to give him up all over again.' She spoke quietly, no trace of accusation in her voice. All the same, the words were like shards of broken glass, slic-ing at his heart.

'That's as may be.'

'Greg, tell me that you're not thinking of leaving again.'

'I don't want to leave you, Jess, that's not what all this is about.'

'Not me. The hospital. Your job.'

'I seem to have two jobs at the moment. I'm not sure how long I can sustain that.'

She just stared at him. Nothing could have hurt Greg

more than her complete, speechless incomprehension. 'Jess, you have to understand.'

'I don't, Greg.' She brushed tears from her eyes. 'But that doesn't mean I won't support you.'

That was something, at least. Perhaps when she'd thought about it a bit, or when she saw the house in Rome? The prospect was remote, but it was a possibility. 'There is something I need some help with.'

She nodded, looking at him solemnly.

'My father left a notebook. I didn't see it when I was here visiting him, but my mother said he showed it to her and told her that it was for me. I can't find it.'

'And you think that it's here somewhere?'

'That's what I'm hoping.'

She straightened, as if at last this was something that she could get to grips with. 'I'll help you look.'

The idea was outrageous. Unthinkable. Greg was far too good a doctor to just give it all up. He loved it too much. He'd never needed to say it, it was clear by the light in his eyes when he brought someone back from the edge. The child had a right to his father's time. The man had a right to pursue his own destiny. It seemed that Greg's father was going to take both of those rights from him.

She wanted to fight for him, but she didn't know how, so she turned her energies to the journal. Leather bound, Greg said, about the size of a paperback book. When he took her into the large library, shelves reaching up to the grand, moulded plaster ceiling, that started to look like finding a needle in a haystack.

'Okay. So why don't you sort the papers that you need to take from here, and I'll look through the books?' She surveyed the task in front of her and swallowed hard.

'You and whose superpowers, Jess?'

'How hard can it be?' She pulled the sleeves of her sweater up to her elbows and found herself suddenly crushed against his chest. 'What's this for?'

'For being too pig-headed to know when to give up.'

'They're only books.' A lot of them. Many leather-bound. Jess wondered what it would be like to have had access to a library like this. No wonder Greg seemed to know so much about so many things.

'And they don't frighten you, eh?' He was hugging her tight. Not the fevered embrace of a lover, just a man who seemed to need some warmth at the moment.

Nothing frightened Jess quite as much as the idea that Greg was thinking about tearing his life to shreds. 'We could narrow it down a bit. If your father was ill, he probably couldn't make it up to the top shelves.' She eyed the tall library steps.

'He could have asked someone to climb up there for him. We had carers here pretty much all the time. And there are the staff in the house, although my mother's given pretty much all of them the third degree and no one seems to have seen the book.'

'Hmm. Suppose I stand on top of the steps and you wheel them along so I don't have to keep running up and down to move them? Would that work?'

'Yeah, it'll work.' He grinned at her. 'You'll have to hang on.'

'Done this before, have you?'

'All the time, when I was a kid.'

'Well, then, you can show me how. Now, let go of me and let's get started.'

CHAPTER SEVEN

THEY WERE OFF the motorway and heading back into London. They'd searched for hours in every place they could think of and hadn't found the notebook. So Greg had loaded two plastic crates of papers into the boot of his car, taken Jess for lunch at the local pub and, in what was fast becoming a private joke between them, given her the car keys.

Jess's phone rang and Greg picked it up from the dashboard. 'It's Gerry.'

'Answer it.' She flashed a grin at him. 'If Gerry's calling me on a Sunday afternoon, it's probably not just for a chat.'

'And I'm answering your phone why?'

'It's my phone. I can ask anyone I like to answer it.' Jess wondered whether Greg would take up the challenge. He could quite easily pretend to press *'reject'* instead of *'answer'* by mistake, and let Jess pull over and call Gerry back.

He grinned, and turned his attention to the phone. 'Gerry? Yes, it's me. No, you can't speak to her, she's driving at the moment. We're not in her car, we're in mine.' He winked at her and held the phone away from his ear. Jess kept her eyes on the road but she could hear a stream of indistinct words from the other end of the line.

'What, you called to tell me this?'

'What's he saying?'

'Nothing of interest. I don't know where he gets the idea that I'm over-particular about my car. What did you call for, Gerry?' He listened intently and then grinned. 'He says there's an emergency heart bypass coming in shortly. If you want to sit in...'

'Yes!' Jess had been waiting for this chance for weeks. 'Tell him yes. If we swing past my place so I can pick up my car...'

'We'll be half an hour. Yes, see you then. Cheers, mate.' He cut the call. 'No point in making a detour all the way over to yours. We'll go straight there.'

'Sure?' Greg answering Gerry's call was one thing, but arriving together at the hospital on a Sunday afternoon looked an awful lot like a public admission that something was going on between them. And Greg had always been so careful to keep his love life well away from his work.

'You're ashamed to be seen with me?' He was grinning.

Hardly. 'I might want to keep you under wraps.' The thought occurred to Jess that she might be happier if he wanted to keep her under wraps. As if his job at the hospital was still a long-term proposition.

'Do you?'

'No.' She didn't care what anyone said, she was proud to be seen with Greg. And if he didn't mind being seen with her...

He nodded, seemingly pleased with what he heard. 'Next left, then. We don't want to get caught in traffic.'

Greg had found himself a cup of coffee and ensconced himself in the back row of the operating theatre viewing gallery. A couple of students sat ready to take notes and Greg ignored their covert glances. Right now they probably reckoned that another few years and they could stop climbing that steep learning curve and relax. He wasn't going to disenchant them.

Jess looked delicious. Scrubbed clean, covered from head to toe in shapeless, sterile theatre garb and concentrating hard on what Gerry was saying to her. He could only see her brow and her eyes, and somehow that was just as enchanting as being able to see everything. Like concentrating on one small part of a magnificent painting, admiring the virtues of a detail to enhance one's appreciation of the whole.

He leaned back in his chair, stretching his legs as much as was possible in the confined space. It would be a while before they were finished, but that was okay. It would be a chance to brush up on his knowledge of a speciality other than his own, and he could watch her. At the moment, a couple of hours where he had a cast-iron excuse to do nothing else except sit and watch Jess seemed like heaven.

He was sprawled on one of the chairs outside the cardiac department when she finally emerged. She looked tired, but her face was one broad sweep of a smile.

'Greg! What are you doing here still?' A trace of guilt intruded on the exhilaration in her eyes. 'I thought you'd gone home.'

'Nothing much to do there.' If you didn't count the boxes of paperwork in his boot. 'I thought I'd stay and watch. You did a good job.' Gerry had given her plenty of opportunity to assist and Jess had come through with flying colours. More than once Greg had seen Gerry's brief nod of approval at her deft, careful work.

'It was really good of Gerry to give me the opportunity.' She looked up at him, her eyes clouded. One of those looks that let Greg know that there was an awful lot of activity going on in her thoughts but gave him no clue about what it was. 'I think I owe you an apology.'

'Do you? What have you done?'

'This morning. I heard you downstairs on the phone.'

'I know.' He stuffed his hands into his jeans pockets. 'I heard you upstairs on the landing.'

'I was cross with you.'

'Yeah, I know that too.' Jess wasn't particularly good at concealing her feelings. He'd never thought that was a bad thing, and his introduction to the business world over the last eight months had only raised that quality in his estimation.

'I should have been a bit more understanding. The way you've been about me wanting to work this afternoon.'

That was the whole thing, in a nutshell. He resented getting out of bed at five in the morning just to settle a dispute between grown men who were only interested in scrambling to gain a bit more territory. Jess had considered this afternoon an opportunity.

'Don't you think this afternoon was worth it?'

'Yes, of course. I'm just saying...'

A pause and a slight grimace that made Greg wonder just how much of this she really believed.

'I'm saying that you've respected what I do. I should do the same and respect what you choose to do.'

Choose was stretching it a bit. The only thing that he had chosen to be was a doctor. And he was still unmoved by any definition of the word 'emergency' that didn't include some pressing threat to life or limb. If Jess thought that the Sunday working she'd done was more important than his, he was inclined to agree with her.

This was a genuine effort to meet him halfway, though. 'Thanks. I appreciate it, Jess. Your support...' Support was probably stretching it a bit as well, he could tell from the look in her eyes. But she nodded.

'I'll take you home.' He pulled the car keys from his pocket.

She hardly hesitated. 'Mmm. Thanks.' She fell into step beside him.

Greg closed his fingers around the car keys, smiling to himself. It was reassuring to be back in the driving seat.

You couldn't really call going out with Greg going out. When their shifts allowed, Jess would go to his flat in the evening and Greg would order some food in from a list of restaurants that seemed to be more than willing to make an exception to the normal insistence on actually turning up and eating on their premises when the name of Greg's father's company was mentioned. Jess could never bring herself to think of it as Greg's company. It was an unknown behemoth that he never talked about but which he seemed to be endlessly thinking about.

When he wasn't eating, he was answering emails. And when he wasn't answering emails, he was apologising for being about to. The long hours between eating and sleeping she spent alone, with just the TV for company. Was this what people meant when they talked about the beginning of the end?

'Can I help you?' Jess had decided to make a change. She'd brought some groceries in for dinner, and cooked for him then stacked the dishwasher while he sat at the kitchen table, staring at his laptop.

'What?'

'Can I help you? I'm a lot faster on a keyboard than you are so you could dictate your emails and I'll type.'

He tore his gaze from the screen for a moment. 'No, honey. Why don't you go and relax in the other room? I won't be long.'

She'd heard that one before, and each time he repeated it, it got just that bit harder to take. 'I'd rather be with you.'

'I have to work.'

'I know. I don't care what I do, I just want to be with you.' The words sounded a bit too much like something a whining girlfriend might say and Jess recoiled from them. 'I might find it interesting.'

He sighed. 'I doubt it. Trust me, it's not riveting stuff.'

That was the worst of it. She could have borne it if Greg was ignoring her in favour of something that was important to him, that he enjoyed. But this was, somehow, the ultimate insult.

Jess turned away, pressing her lips together. She should be supportive. She *wanted* to be supportive. But it was difficult when she had no idea where she stood with Greg.

'Can't I just have a minute? There's something I want to ask you.'

'Of course.' A couple of keystrokes saved whatever it was that he was doing, and he closed the lid of his laptop. 'I'm all yours.'

He wasn't, but the look on his face made Jess's world suddenly tilt. The worries, the nagging doubts, the questions about whether Greg really wanted to spend time with her or not all slid to the back of her consciousness and were replaced by that smile. The one that seemed to tell her everything she needed to know.

'I know you're busy, Greg. Why don't you let me do the model of the hospital? Or I can find someone else to do it. I was talking to Ash the other day and he said he'd help.'

'Ash?' He raised one eyebrow. 'The young guy in Orthopaedics?'

'He's the same age as me. And he's just split up with his girlfriend so he's got a bit of time on his hands.' Jess tailed off as Greg's brow darkened. That was just crazy.

Ash was good looking, fun to have around and could no more measure up to Greg than any other man she'd ever met. 'What?'

'Nothing.' He scrubbed his hand across his face. 'I suppose you're right. But…'

'But what?' Jess wasn't going to let him go back to work now. There was already too much that was being left unsaid between them.

'I promised you that I'd do it.' A quirk of a smile and suddenly he was back with her, his dark eyes seeming to see nothing else. 'I might start getting jealous if you and Ash disappear off together to build my model.'

'Jealous? Are you?' What the hell was she doing? She hated mind games and had no time for jealousy, particularly when it wasn't warranted. But suddenly Greg seemed to have started taking notice of her, and she was desperate for even these crumbs of his attention.

He saw through her in a moment. 'You think I don't have it in me to be jealous?'

'Just testing.' She broke off as he leaned over, his lips finding hers. Gentle hands, propelling her to her feet and then backwards. He perched her on the counter top, sliding his hips between her knees.

'Getting any answers?' One hand cupped her cheek and Jess struggled for control then gave up as pleasure oozed across her skin.

'Yeah.'

'What are they?' He pulled her tight against his body and she gasped. Nuzzling at her neck, he whispered into her ear, 'What are they, Jess?'

She was trembling. She wanted to tell Greg that the only thing she wanted was a little more of his time, his attention, but that seemed like a recipe for disaster. Her mother had always told her that you never begged a man for more of anything and she'd never questioned that. Suddenly it occurred to Jess that she might be about to beg, and she wondered whether her mother had done the same with her father.

'The only answer I have is that I must be getting a little crazy. I'm not going to play any more games with you just to get your attention. I'd rather just walk out of here now.'

He was suddenly still. 'You have my attention.'

Not for long, though. She felt as if she was on a ship, pitching in a storm. Sliding helplessly between doubt and love as the deck tilted back and forth beneath her. 'Do I?'

He stepped back, planting his hands on the counter top to either side of her, eyes clouded with frustration. 'What do you want from me, Jess?'

Frankly she had no idea. She wanted more than her father had given her mother. That was about as far as Jess had ever really considered the matter. 'This is not how I thought we'd be, Greg.'

'I can't do anything about that right now.' He turned away from her abruptly, leaving Jess to push herself down from her perch on the counter top.

'You always have a choice, Greg.'

'Yeah? What choice do I have? You don't seem to understand, Jess.'

The world tilted again and this time Jess was slammed hard against a wall of anger. 'Trying to understand is all I've been doing for the last few weeks. If you're too busy for me then you should just say so and stop stringing me along.'

He rounded on her. 'Oh, so I'm stringing you along now, am I? You don't think much of me, do you?'

'I'm not saying that's what you mean to do.'

He gave a short bark of a laugh. 'Well, that makes me feel so much better. I might be callous, but that's okay because I'm so knuckle-headed that I'm not aware of what I'm doing.' He marched over to the kitchen cupboard, seeming to need to do something. Flipping it open, he banged two cups down onto the counter.

'That's not what I said. If you want to think that about yourself, be my guest. But don't you dare put those words into my mouth.'

He didn't turn. He seemed to have switched into auto-pilot, reaching up for the coffee and measuring the last of the packet into the machine, spilling some as he did so. Jess huffed with frustration. 'Can't you at least look at me? We had coffee ten minutes ago.'

He slung the empty coffee packet into the sink, along with the measuring spoon. When he turned, his gaze was cold, proud, but there was something hot-blooded about it that made Jess shiver.

'I never chose to have anything to do with Shaw Industries, but I've been given that responsibility, and I can't walk away from it. That's all it is. This is not about you and me.'

'But it affects you and me.' That was about as close as Jess's pride would allow her to get to asking him for more.

'I'm not going to make any promises I can't keep, Jess. I have no idea how long this is all going to take. I wish things were different, but they're not.'

'You can't just allow it to take you over, Greg. At some point you're going to have to decide where your own priorities lie.'

He let out a short, sharp breath. A gesture of helplessness that told Jess he was out of ideas on this one. This seemed to be tearing him up inside. More precisely, *she* seemed to be tearing him up...

'Perhaps we should take a break. Just a couple of weeks to figure things out.'

He stared at her. Clearly Jess wasn't the only one who was having trouble believing that she was saying this. But they both needed a little space, to sort their own issues out, before they ripped each other to bits.

'A break. You mean we should call it a day?'

'No. I mean a break. A couple of weeks to take the pressure off. Work things out.' Right now, looking at him, it was impossible to credit that *'goodbye'* should feature anywhere in this. Ever.

Her heart was yelling at him to say no. To turn his back on the seemingly hundreds of people who waited for him in a not so orderly queue, out there in cyberspace. If he offered to take the night off, just this once, she'd say yes in a heartbeat.

'Perhaps you're right.' She felt his hand on her arm. So nearly enough to make her stay and yet so far from what she needed right now. 'I'll take you home.'

He really hadn't been paying attention. 'I've got my car with me tonight. I brought some shopping in, remember?' Jess wondered whether he'd get around to restocking the fridge after she was gone. Probably not. At least he had enough in there to last for a while, though.

'Yeah, of course. I'm sorry about all this, Jess.' He scraped his hand across his face and she almost relented. But if she did that, they'd only be having this same argument again soon.

'Don't be. We're just taking some time off, eh?' So why did this seem so final? Perhaps because there was no way back for Jess now, unless he gave a little. And she wasn't sure that he'd do that.

He walked with her to the lift and they rode down to the car park in silence. Greg watched her to her car gave her a wave and turned back into the lift. It appeared he wasn't going to watch her go. Jess waited, gripping the steering-wheel, her gaze fixed on him as he jabbed the call button for the lift. He wasn't going to look back. She started the engine and drove out of the car park, revving the engine into rather more of a roar than was strictly necessary. His mind was probably already on the problems that waited for him upstairs and he hadn't even heard her go either.

Greg kept his finger on the lift button, ignoring the insistent 'ding' that accompanied the twitch of the doors as the machine hinted to him ever so gently that there were probably people waiting on other floors and they should get going now. He heard her car slow as she approached the ramp up to street level and turned when he was sure that she could no longer see him in her rear-view mirror.

He didn't blame her for what she'd done. It would have taken considerably less neglect on Jess's part before Greg would have considered himself hard done by and left. There was nothing to say either in his own defence or in terms of promises for the future. He'd heard enough promises from his father to know just how much damage a broken one could cause. But things would change. She'd see.

CHAPTER EIGHT

JESS HAD BEEN trying very hard not to miss Greg for almost two weeks. It had been a stupid argument, she'd said things she hadn't really meant, and she guessed that he had too. But the main stumbling block remained. Was she just the latest in a long string of girlfriends that Greg had loved then lost interest in? If so, she couldn't bring herself to tell him that this one still loved him.

She had other things to think about, though. Like getting through the day, doing her job the best she could and smiling as if nothing had happened. Ignoring the nagging thought that her body's monthly rhythm had missed a beat. It was nothing. She'd been working hard, sleeping badly and not eating properly, that was all.

Today had been a busy day, but she'd kept on top of things and it seemed that she'd be leaving work on time tonight. And then, at five-thirty on the dot, the department secretary paged her.

'What have you got for me, Bev?' By the time she got down to the office she'd convinced herself that she didn't really want to go home after all.

'Some people were looking for you. I asked them to go to the waiting room.'

'Who? I didn't have a clinic today.'

Beverly shook her head. 'No, I think they might know you. One of them is a doctor.'

'Who is he?'

'No idea. But he's got that doctor's look about him.' Beverly tapped the side of her nose. 'Interested instead of nervous. They're in the waiting room.'

The waiting room was deserted, apart from a couple sitting in one corner. Something like foreboding prickled at the back of Jess's neck.

'Rosa. Ted.' She sat down in the chair opposite them. 'How nice to see you both.' What were they doing here?

Rosa smiled. That self-possessed, gracious smile that somehow managed to be genuine as well. 'It's good to see you too, Jess.' She looked around the waiting room. 'This is very nice.'

'Yes, they renovated the whole department a couple of years ago. Much brighter than it used to be.' Jess flipped a querying glance towards Ted.

'We were looking for Greg. You haven't seen him, have you?' Ted got straight to the point and Jess heaved a sigh of relief. For a moment there she'd thought that Greg might have told them about the things she'd said and they were here to remonstrate with her.

'Isn't he down in A and E? I haven't spoken to him today.' Okay, so not for two weeks. But there was something the matter, and suddenly that was of no consequence. It didn't matter if she hadn't spoken to him for two years, she'd still be there for him.

'No, we went there first.' Rosa shrugged, letting go with just a hint of well-manicured exasperation.

'And we didn't hang around because they were busy.' Ted had clearly guided his wife up here before she'd got in the way. 'Rosa's tried his mobile and his home phone.'

'He doesn't answer. His mobile's switched off,' Rosa finished for him.

Greg never switched his mobile off. The prickle at the back of Jess's neck got worse and she tried to shrug it off. 'He should be here. But he has another mobile. He uses it for work. His other work, I mean.' She wasn't sure quite what to call it.

Rosa nodded, pursing her lips. 'Shaw Industries.'

'Yes. But I don't know the number.' Jess hadn't wanted to know it. She'd tried staring at the sleek, black handset a number of times in the hope that it might dissolve into thin air, but that hadn't worked either.

Ted's relaxed, even-handedness broke in. 'We were wondering whether you could find out where he is for us. They looked very busy in A and E and we didn't want to interrupt them.' Rosa nodded, thin-lipped.

'Yes, of course.' Jess could get the information easily from the receptionist. 'He's probably on his break or something. Wait here, I'll find out for you.'

Jess hurried down to A and E, taking in the canteen on the way. Greg wasn't there either. But the receptionist knew exactly where he was. Jess walked back up to the cardiology waiting room, feeling a little sick.

'Rosa, I'm sorry, but he's not here. He's got a few days off this week.' And next week. She'd wanted Greg to cut back on work, but it had never occurred to her that he might choose Shaw Industries over his work here at the hospital.

Rosa rolled her eyes and made a gesture that defied translation but implied an immediate understanding of the situation. 'I'll find him.' She looked at her watch and pulled her mobile out of her bag, scrolling through the contacts list.

Ted took the phone from her hand. 'Not here, darling.'

He stood, waiting for Rosa to follow him. 'We're sorry to have bothered you, Jess.'

'It's no trouble.' Jess wasn't going to let them walk out on her now. 'I'll take you down to the canteen. You can get a cup of tea and make your call there.'

Ted asked whether there was anywhere else that Jess needed to be, and then insisted she join them. Rosa was on the phone almost as soon as she sat down.

'Pat? It's Rosa. How are you?' Rosa smiled into the phone. 'Really? You must give us a call when you arrive and come over for dinner. That would be perfect. I wondered whether you've heard from Greg today?'

Jess smiled. The ladylike version of taking Pat by the throat, shaking her and demanding to know where he was.

'Is he? No, that's all right, thank you, it's not important. I'll catch up with him.' Rosa's smile drained rapidly from her face as she cut the call. 'He's at the London office. A board meeting. He won't be finished until late if I know anything about these things.'

Jess took a sip of her tea to steady her. 'I'm sorry, I didn't know. I haven't seen Greg for a couple of weeks. Things have been…um…difficult.'

Ted came to the rescue again. 'That's a shame. We were thinking, hoping, that he'd not been in touch because he was spending time with you.'

'No. He's been working.' Jess chanced a look at Rosa and saw only understanding in her face.

Ted leaned back in his chair, smiling at his wife. 'Well, I suppose we should go and do that Christmas shopping, then. No point in wasting a journey.'

'But…' Rosa puffed out a breath. 'I suppose so.' She pulled a flat package, wrapped in brown paper, out of her handbag. 'Unless this fits through his letter-box.'

Ted scratched his nose. 'I doubt it.'

Jess stared at the package. 'The book. You've found his father's book.' Greg had said his mother had been searching diligently for it, and she must have found it.

'Yes. You'll never guess where it was.' She paused and Jess shook her head. 'It was in the tower. There's a big old chest in there, full of goodness knows what, and it had been slipped inside there.'

'And his father put it in there for him to find.'

'Yes.' Rosa twitched the corners of her mouth down. 'Although how much good it's going to be…'

'Greg's father had a secondary brain tumour. Quite a large one.' There was only compassion in Ted's face.

'Which might have affected his language functions.' Jess could imagine Greg's disappointment if the book was unintelligible.

Ted nodded. 'It seems that it did. Damn shame. We thought it would be better to deliver it personally under the circumstances.'

Rosa nodded. 'Silly really. I should have called first.'

'If you had, he wouldn't have answered. And we'd have come anyway.' Ted brushed away the wasted journey as if it was nothing. 'Jess, would it be inappropriate of us to ask whether you'll be seeing Greg in the next few days? If not, we can give him a call tomorrow evening and he can come up and collect the book on Sunday.'

She might not be going out with Greg any more but she could still be a friend to him. She knew how much he'd wanted to find the book and she couldn't bear the thought of him waiting and worrying about what it contained.

'I can take the book. I'll give him a call tomorrow morning, and if he's at home I'll pop it round in my lunch hour.'

'We don't want to put you to any trouble.' Rosa's eyes flashed with gratitude.

'You're not. I'll take good care of it. I know how important it is.'

'That's kind of you, Jess, thank you.' Ted took the parcel from his wife and handed it over to Jess.

'This was his last chance, wasn't it?'

Rosa nodded. 'Yes. He didn't say so, but I think he was hoping that his father might have written some of the things he never said to him.' She grimaced. 'He didn't. I never really thought he would. John was always too involved with his work.'

Like father, like son. Jess hoped not, for Greg's sake.

'So…' Ted drank the last dregs of his tea. 'Jess, have you finished for the day?'

'Pretty much. I just have to check in and make sure there's nothing else for me and then I'll be going home.'

'That's perfect. I'll have another cup of this gorgeous hospital tea and we'll take you for dinner. If you're free, that is?'

Of course she was free. And she couldn't deny that she wanted some company tonight. 'Or we could do a bit of shopping first? The shops are all open late for Christmas.' She glanced at Rosa, who brightened visibly. Jess had imagined that shopping would cheer her up a little.

Ted rolled his eyes, chuckling. 'Thought I was going to get out of that. Okay, we'll shop and then we'll eat.'

CHAPTER NINE

JESS HAD CALLED. She'd managed to talk Gerry into giving her a long lunch hour and she'd be here in…Greg looked at his watch…about ten minutes.

He scanned the living room. His cleaning lady had been in yesterday and everything was neat and in its place. His laptop was hidden away in the TV cabinet, and he'd bundled everything that had anything to do with Shaw Industries into plastic crates, stacked them in the store cupboard in the hall and locked the door.

He began to pace the full length of the hallway, looking at his watch as he did so. She had to come. If she didn't, he'd do what he'd originally planned, go and find her and tell her that things would be different from now on.

The intercom buzzed and he jerked round so quickly that he almost pulled a muscle in his back. He forgot all about waiting for a few seconds, to make out that he hadn't been waiting in the hallway for her, and punched the button to release the entrance doors downstairs.

A pause and then a quiet knock on the door.

'Hey.' Suddenly the last two weeks seemed like nothing. She was here, her face glowing as if it was Christmas Day. This *was* Christmas Day, as far as Greg was concerned. 'Come in.'

He remembered to stand back from the doorway and

she smiled at him—he'd so missed that smile—and walked past him into the hallway. He'd missed her scent too, to the point that it seemed to haunt him, clinging to pillows and sheets, even though they were fresh on the bed.

'What have I done to deserve this?' He wondered if he should kiss her and decided it was taking too much for granted.

'I have something for you. I have to warn you that it's probably going to be a disappointment.' She handed him a flat brown paper parcel.

That was okay, she was here, and that was all that really mattered. 'What is it?'

'It's your father's book. Rosa found it. She and Ted were at the hospital yesterday but you weren't around and they came up to Cardiology.'

Greg stared at the package. Suddenly he didn't want to open it. 'And they gave it to you?'

'Yes. I said I'd bring it to you. We did some shopping and had dinner.'

He'd been missing her like the feeling was going out of fashion, and she'd been swanning around going shopping with his mother? Fury tore at Greg's chest and he turned on his heel, marching into the sitting room and slinging the parcel down onto the coffee table.

He heard her behind him. 'What? What's wrong now?'

'Nothing…nothing. I'm sorry, Jess, yesterday was a long day. Thanks for bringing this round.' He turned, smiling as best he could. She'd be off now, as that was all she'd come for.

'Aren't you going to open it?' She stared pointedly at the package.

'No. I'll do that later. I've some things to do. You'll be wanting to get back as well.' He moved to usher her back towards the doorway but she evaded him.

'I've taken a long lunch hour. I told you that.' She took her coat off and sat down on the sofa, plumping her handbag defiantly onto the floor.

'You've done what you came to do.' He couldn't help the anger in his voice.

'Think so?' She jutted her chin at him and he almost melted. Almost.

'You've delivered the book. Is there anything else?'

'Yes.' She sprang to her feet and marched over to him. 'Just this.'

She raised her arm and for a moment Greg thought she might be about to slap him. He stood his ground, reckoning that he probably didn't deserve much better from her, and felt her hand on the back of his neck, pulling him roughly towards her.

She kissed him. Wild and warm and angry. Deep, passionate and finally tender. Just as he began to reach for her, she was gone, picking up her coat and huffing in annoyance as she tried to thread her hand through one of the tangled sleeves.

Oh, no, she didn't. If she thought she was going to leave now... Greg covered the floor between them in three strides and caught her by the arm. She spun round and he pinned her against him. 'What was that for?'

She turned her face up towards him, defiance blazing in her eyes. 'You can tell me to go now, and I'll go. But I'm not leaving without letting you know how I feel.'

'I don't want you to go, Jess.'

He backed her against the sofa, almost collapsing on top of her as she lost her balance and fell onto the cushions. This time he kissed her. Anger and passion again, melting together into an explosive cocktail. She moved beneath him, a little cry escaping her lips, and her sweetness almost overwhelmed him. How he'd missed her.

That heavy-lidded, golden look almost destroyed him. He murmured her name, and she seemed to melt into him, as if there was no such thing as him or her, only them.

'I missed you, Jess.'

She hesitated. Silently he willed her to say it. 'I missed you too.'

Triumph shimmered through him, teasing every nerve ending. He should let her up now, but somehow he couldn't. Not until she kissed him again.

She didn't make him wait. Her kiss still had a trace of defiance, a dash of anger, but this time it was assured. The way he wanted her to feel with him.

'One more thing.'

'What's that?' She was smiling now.

He leaned in until his lips were almost touching her ear. 'Do you have a right to my attention?'

Her beautiful eyes clouded in doubt. He hated that he'd been a part of creating that doubt. 'Do you, Jess?'

'Yes? I do?'

He felt himself smile inside. 'Right answer. Only you could be more definite about it…'

'Could I?'

'Yes. It's the truth, and I need you to know it.'

She thought for a moment. 'Let me up, Greg.'

Damn! She wasn't going to say it. Greg shifted, sitting up, and she followed, sitting close, smiling when he put his arm around her.

'I have a right to expect your attention.' She whispered the words into his ear.

He chuckled. 'Was that so difficult?'

She rocked her head from side to side, as if weighing it up. 'Surprisingly easy.'

He wondered how long she had before she had to go back to work. Actually, it didn't matter. He'd say what he had to say if he had to follow her back, and gabble it into her ear in the lift up to Cardiology. 'If I sounded a bit gruff…over you going shopping with my mother…'

She made a face. 'Somewhere between noticeable disapproval and overt censure. Just to let you know, we didn't talk about you, or us.'

That only made things worse. Greg swallowed his disappointment. 'Rub it in, why don't you? Just when I was coming to terms with feeling left out.'

'Ah. Well then, we did talk about you a bit. Only I can't tell you about that, because Rosa was buying Christmas presents. Anyway, don't you hate shopping?' She smiled up at him, that beguiling, mischievous look flickering in her eyes. Jess had a way of making everything seem right.

'Well, Ted and I might have made a few faces at each other.' Even so, he liked the thought of watching Jess and his mother, discussing their purchases, deciding for and then against, laughing together at the brightly lit counters, ablaze with Christmas decorations. He could have carried her bags, shepherded her through the crowds in the shops and on the pavements.

'There you are, then. Anyway, shopping's a pretty cutthroat business at this time of the year.'

'Jess?'

'Yes?'

'Come back to me.'

'I… We…' There was only one answer that Jess could give to that. There had only ever been one answer where Greg was concerned. If she didn't give it immediately, it was only because she wanted so badly to do it right this time. 'Do you really think this is the right thing, Greg?'

His chest rose and fell in a short, explosive laugh. 'As a friend, I'd tell you that waiting around for any guy is bad news. That you deserve a lot better than someone who's fighting to keep his head above water and can't always give you the attention you deserve.'

'Yeah. And?'

'As a lover, I'll say that I'm a pretty miserable excuse for a suitor. That sometimes I get distracted, and I feel guilty about that and lash out at you, instead of doing what I should and telling you that I'm sorry. But you always have my heart, I promise you that.'

'You'd better make up your mind which you are, then.' Choose right. She was willing him to choose right.

'Are you free tomorrow?' Warmth filtered back into his tone.

'Yes. What about you? There's a whole twenty-four hours for Shaw Industries to come up with something that's more important.'

'I'll be there. I promise.'

'It's a date, then.' It was almost impossible to keep from smiling when his voice caressed her like this. Liquid caramel. Jess tried to think of something else but the only alternative she could come up with at the moment was melted chocolate.

'What time shall I pick you up? Is five o'clock too early?'

'No, that'll be great. I've got to pop into the hospital, take a look in the library to see if they've got any of the books we need for the storytellers, so perhaps I could do that first and then come straight over to you?'

'Why don't I meet you there? At about three o'clock. I could give you a hand.'

Pure, unadulterated happiness crashed over her, like a wave. Bubbling around her and then pulling her under. 'I'd really like that.'

He smiled. That slow, delicious smile that just kept on giving. 'When do you have to be back at work?'

'About thirty-five minutes. I have to go soon.'

'If I drove you back, it'd only take ten minutes.' He wound his arms around her waist, pulling her close again.

'I can stay if you want some company. I'll make a cup of coffee and you can take a quick look at the book.' She gestured towards the package on the table.

He shook his head. 'That can wait. I, on the other hand, have already waited long enough. I just want to hold you for a little while longer.' He kissed her and every nerve ending flared abruptly into life. Suddenly there was nothing else in the world that she needed to do as much as kiss him back.

'I'm sorry, Greg. I shouldn't have—'

He laid his finger across her lips. 'Hey. None of that. We are what we are. Everyone has issues. But we can work through them. We've just got to keep talking.'

'And?'

'When we've finished with the talking, we could try a little loving.'

'Just a little?'

He chuckled. 'Not if I have any say in the matter.'

CHAPTER TEN

THE HOSPITAL LIBRARY wasn't large, but it did have as many bookshelves as could be squeezed into such a limited space, and they were all full. Greg found Jess in there, poring over a list and consulting the shelves.

'Hey, there. Any luck?'

She shrugged. 'Not sure yet. None of this is any particular order. People just take books out and put them back anywhere.' She paused, grinning, and pulled a volume from a pile on the floor. 'Ooh, look! There's a good start.'

'A Christmas Carol.' Greg took the book from her and flipped the pages. 'You know, I don't think I've ever actually read this. I've seen films, of course.'

'Then you should take it home. Might get you into the spirit of things.' She smiled at him, and Greg's world tipped slightly. He could almost see himself taking time out to actually do some reading.

He put the book aside for later. 'I've got something for you. A surprise.'

Her eyes flipped to his empty hands and then to his face. 'A surprise? What is it?'

'Well, if I walked in here holding it, it wouldn't be a surprise, would it? Anyway, first things first.'

Her ability to anticipate what he wanted was almost uncanny. She was in his arms almost before he'd had a chance to reach for her. Her kiss told him that everything his senses had been yearning for was right there. Not yet, though. He wasn't going to blow it by forgetting to say any of the things he'd left unspoken up till now.

'You look lovely.' She was dressed simply, dark trousers and a red sweater. A complicated twist of beads around her neck that weren't quite her style but looked great. 'You smell gorgeous. Did you dress up for me?'

She flushed awkwardly then met his gaze. 'Yes, I did.'

'I appreciate that.' He kissed her again. That physical language that meant more than words sometimes.

She nodded, eyes glistening. 'So where's my surprise?' She dug him in the ribs. 'Come on.'

He chuckled, breaking away from her and fetching the box that he'd left in the hallway, setting it down on the small library table. She gave him a questioning look then tore off the packing tape with which he'd resealed the box and pulled out layers of bubble wrap.

'Greg! It's…' She peered into the box. 'Look at the roof and the little chimneys.'

He reached inside and carefully drew the model out. 'You like it?'

'It's beautiful. Look, there's even grass in the courtyard and a little gatehouse and railings.' She was entranced, trying to take in all the features of the tiny representation of the hospital at once. 'What did you do?'

'I didn't make it myself, if that's what you mean. There's a company that Shaw Industries uses that make models of some of our larger engineering installations. I passed the job on to them and tipped the wink to Ash that he wouldn't need to do anything. Do you mind?'

'If you think I'm going to quibble about how you got your contribution to the pageant done…' she shrugged

'…I've been begging for things for months now. I'm not picky about where they come from.'

'Good. So, can I expect a—?'

She went to kiss him before he could even ask. Greg backed her against a free-standing bookcase, which wobbled precariously, so he changed direction, steering her against one of the wall cabinets. Holding back from her, letting their lips just touch.

It was all that was needed to start the long, slow burn that would build through the rest of the afternoon and most of the evening, until they had a chance to quench it. That might take most of the night.

He kissed her again, this time a little deeper. Or maybe it was Jess who did that. One of the things he loved about making love with her was that he was never really sure who was doing what for whom. Everything just flowed, one caress into another, without thought or artifice, pleasuring both of them in equal measure.

'We'd better be getting on, then.' He had no intention of leaving her satisfied. Not yet. Not for a long time.

'Yeah. There's a lot to do.' Her hand nudged the top of his leg and he shuddered. The trouble with Jess was that she could play this game so much better than he could.

He gave up and reached for the list, keeping one arm coiled around her shoulders. 'You know, I reckon most of these books are in the library at my father's house.' He still couldn't quite bring himself to call it his own. 'Can you do with some extra copies?'

'Yes. I need to get as many as possible. I've got a lot of volunteers for the storytelling.'

'So why don't you send the list to my mother and she'll sort them out and box them up? I'll be up there some time before Christmas and I can pick them up.'

'Would she mind? I'll make sure I get them back to you.'

Greg laughed. 'No, she'll be very happy about that. She called me last night and asked me whether I was considering being a total ass and ignoring you for much longer.'

'What did you tell her?'

'I told her I'm not considering that.'

She gave a small nod. 'Are we going to be okay, Greg?' The way she looked at him, in almost agonised belief that he could make everything all right, wrenched his heart.

'We're working on it, honey. Together.'

'Yes.' That seemed to be enough for her, and she took refuge in his arms, pressing her cheek against his chest. She trusted him. He would do all he could not to let her down.

He kissed her lightly on the lips. 'So, as we're here to work, what do you want me to do?'

She laughed. Soft, sweet laughter, like an angel caressing his senses. 'Sort out some of these books for me.'

The restaurant he took her to was only ten minutes' walk from the hospital, along a little cobbled alleyway by the river. Jess hadn't even known it was there, and guessed that it didn't need to advertise itself too much. A small foyer, where they were stripped of their coats, and up a flight of stairs into an understated but noticeably classy eating area. Waiters, who appeared and disappeared as if they'd just walked out of the walls, and a no-frills menu that clearly underplayed some very haute cuisine.

The first course came and was cleared away, waiters melting in and out of the space around their table like wraiths who knew exactly when to appear and when to tactfully disappear. Jess had asked about Greg's father's book, expecting him to shrug it off, keep his feelings close to his chest, but instead he sent one of the waiters downstairs to fetch it from his coat.

'Can I look?' Jess was unsure just how much he wanted to share.

He nodded. 'Yes. I'd like you to, if you don't mind.'

It was the first time he'd let her see anything to do with his father or Shaw Industries. Jess's hand shook as she flipped through the pages, full of closely written paragraphs and complex diagrams. This wasn't what she had expected. 'He's written something.'

'Yeah. Look a little closer.'

At first glance the text almost looked as if it should make sense. But when Jess scanned the pages more closely, she saw that Greg meant. Disjointed phrases, flashes, impressions that dangled the promise of some kind of meaning, but at the same time fell short of conveying anything. A chart that must have meant something but had no labels.

'I'm sorry, Greg. I know how much you wanted this to be something.'

He shrugged. 'I shouldn't have got my hopes up. He couldn't communicate with me when he was alive and he sure as hell can't do it now.'

Anger flashed across his face. Good. That was good. She'd rather see Greg rage at this than just coldly accept it.

'Isn't there anything in here that makes any sense?' She turned the pages slowly, looking for something, anything, that might be an intelligible message.

'Not to me. He shook his head. 'Maybe he didn't know what it meant either.'

'At least he tried.'

A short bark of a laugh. 'You always think the best of people.'

'Is that such a bad thing?'

He scrubbed his hand across his eyes. 'Not at all. Just saying.'

Jess's eye lit on a phrase. 'Look.' She laid the book on

the table, facing him. 'See what it says there? "Son is here."
That's on the previous page, too. He knew you were there
for him and that obviously meant something.'

'Yeah. Although he couldn't remember my name.'

Enough of this. 'You know better than that, Greg.' She
sought his gaze and held it. Perhaps she was expecting too
much. 'It's natural that you should feel that way as his son.
As a doctor, it's my place to tell you that he might not have
been able to vocalise his feelings but they were still there.'

'You're right. I know. I just can't feel that way at the
moment.'

'You will, in time. The tumour was obviously affecting
the language centres of his brain. It may be that someone
with specific expertise in this area would be able to help.'

'Do you think there's any point?'

'I don't know. I just think that you can't give up on him
now.' Jess might mistrust John Shaw's intentions but she
loved Greg. If she had to deal with the father to help the
son, she'd do it.

He nodded. 'I just wish he'd been able to give me a few
ideas about the right thing to do next.'

'Maybe he trusted you. He might have reckoned that
you'd make the right decisions all on your own.'

Greg stared at her. 'I...I don't think...' He shrugged,
summoning up a smile. 'I don't think that's something that
ever occurred to me.'

'Maybe you should give it some thought.'

'Maybe.' Greg closed the book and threw his napkin
over it, as if that was an end to it and even looking at the
volume was hard for him. 'Ah. Here's our pudding.'

One of the waiters appeared out of thin air, where he
seemed to have been hovering, waiting for them to finish talking. Laying their plates in front of them, he disappeared again.

'Where do they go?' Jess leaned across the table con-spiratorially.

Greg laughed. 'It's all done with trapdoors and pulleys. Do you like it here?'

'Yeah, I do, actually.' If he'd told her about this place before they'd come, she'd have turned it down out of hand. But now that she was here it wasn't so bad. She felt relaxed, comfortable and the food was wonderful. She probed her chocolate pudding with her spoon. 'This looks lovely.'

'Yeah. Wish I'd gone for it.' He reached out towards her plate and Jess rapped his spoon with hers.

'Don't you dare. Anyway, the lemon meringue looks nice too.'

He took a mouthful. 'Yes. It's very good. So we'll come back here some time?'

They were grinning at each other across the table. 'Yes. Only next week we go to Aldo's.' Diners lined up at tres-tle tables, waiters who tapped their feet and stared at the ceiling if you didn't order quickly enough, and a good, filling meal.

'Okay. I like Aldo's.' He nodded and left her to tuck into the best chocolate pudding she'd ever tasted.

She woke up in his arms. Jess took a moment to appreciate the novelty of not having to wonder where Greg was, and then stretched a little, just to test whether he was awake or not. His hand wandered sleepily to her stomach and stayed there.

Last night had been perfect. Enough to drive every one of her misgivings from her head, along with every other worry. Taking his hand in hers and pulling it close to her heart, she drifted back to sleep.

When she woke again something was wrong. The room

was swimming and almost before her eyes were open properly she was on her feet and running for the bathroom.

'Are you okay, Jess?'

The vomiting was sudden and violent, but at least it passed as quickly as it had come, and by the time Greg made the bathroom, she was already rinsing her mouth.

'Yeah.' She was still shivering, cold sweat on her brow, and Greg wrapped her in his dressing gown, guiding her back to the bed.

'Here, lie down for a minute.' He propped the pillows up and she relaxed back into them, wishing that they'd swallow her up. Not quite the awakening she'd been planning on treating him to.

'Can I get you something? A glass of water?'

'No. Thanks, I'm okay.' She shrugged. 'Don't know what happened there.' Though she was beginning to fathom it out and she tried to ignore the conclusion that was staring her in the face.

Greg's face was clouded in thought. Apparently he too was beginning to fathom it out. 'How late are you?'

'What? Who says...?'

'How late?' His voice was firm, almost as if he was talking to a difficult patient.

'Don't be like this, Greg.' He couldn't know. She didn't even know so how could he possibly know?

'Okay, then. You can clear this up in a second. All you have to do is tell me that I'm imagining things.'

'You're...' She couldn't. Or, if he was, then it looked as if he was imagining the same things that she was. The things that she'd, put down to stress and the missed meals and sleepless nights of the last two weeks.

'Jess, stop this. You refused any wine last night, you're sick this morning. What's going on?'

'Nothing. Nothing. I just didn't want the wine. It smelled a bit off.'

'It was fine.'

'Maybe it's just a stomach bug.'

'How late?'

'Two weeks. And a couple of days.'

'How many days?' His voice was gentle, but Jess didn't dare look up into his face.

'Four.'

'Is that usual for you?'

'No, I'm… You can usually set your watch by my monthly cycle.'

'I'm assuming you haven't done a test?'

'No. I thought I was just a bit run down.'

'This isn't like you, Jess.' He wrapped his arms around her, letting out a long sigh. 'A test would only take five minutes and then we'd know.'

'Yes. Then we'd know.' What if she didn't want to know just yet? She might just want to hang onto the possibility that she was right, without having to actually face any of the hard questions that was going to pose. But now that Greg was involved, it changed everything. 'I'll stop on my way home and get a test kit from the chemist.'

'Jess.' He let out a huff of exasperation. 'Okay, this is what we're going to do. I'll pop out now to the all-night chemist and get a test kit. Then we'll get it done, and… well, we can work out what comes next when we know what the result is.'

Somewhere, deep inside, she was glad. Glad that Greg had forced the issue. That he'd been stronger than she was, and that he'd cared enough to be gentle, too. 'Yes. All right.'

He reached for her, grasping her by the shoulders and looking straight into her face. A pulse beat at the side of his brow. He wasn't as calm as he sounded. 'It'll be okay, Jess. We'll work this out together.'

She gulped back the tears. He was sticking by her, this far at least. Or perhaps he was just taking control. She preferred the former.

'Okay?' He wasn't going anywhere until she gave him a 'yes'.

'Yes. Okay.'

CHAPTER ELEVEN

GREG IGNORED THE smile from the woman behind the counter at the chemist. She probably had him down as a guy who couldn't wait to become a father. In truth, if he'd had the first idea about how to be a father he might have had a clue about what he wanted. Currently he had neither.

Jess was sitting up in his bed when he got back, toying with one of the dry crackers he'd got for her, his dressing gown wrapped tightly around her. He laid the paper bag down next to her and she hesitated, then snatched it up and made for the bathroom. He heard the door close and then the click of the lock.

Ten minutes and not a sound had come from the other side of the bathroom door. Jess supposed that she should go out and face him. Not yet.

Not yet.

She stood up from her perch on the side of the bath. She didn't feel any different. Looked in the mirror. She didn't look any different either.

'It's all right. It's going to be all right.' She whispered the words to her own reflection, and received a smile in response. It was going to be all right.

Her hand wandered to her stomach. Still flat, no signs yet. 'Hey, baby.' Her first words to her unborn child. 'Your mother loves you. Everything's going to be just fine.' It didn't seem odd to be talking like this. In the last ten minutes her world had turned upside down, split apart at the seams, and she'd fallen hopelessly and irrevocably in love with the scrap of life inside her.

Would her baby—their baby, she supposed—be like him? Would some accident of genetics mean that it grew into an olive-skinned, dark-eyed charmer? Strong and tall, owing nothing to its mother? She rubbed her stomach, letting the thought percolate for a while. She liked it rather better than she was ready to admit.

What would Greg say? Would he wonder if she'd somehow meant this to happen? He was a rich man, and most women would jump at the chance to snare him. Slowly but surely everything began to unravel. All the promises they'd made in the last few days. Then they'd had the luxury of being able to live with uncertainty. Things were different now.

'He can keep his money.' She mouthed the words at the mirror, in case he was outside, listening. 'We can do without it.'

A tap sounded at the door. 'Jess?'

She jumped guiltily and whirled round. Another tap, louder this time. 'Jess? Are you waiting for me to break the door down?'

She couldn't help smiling. A part of her wanted him to do just that. Pull her into his arms and protect her from all the monsters that were out there in the dark. Take her to live in his gilded castle, where he'd make her his queen and love her always.

She gulped in a breath. 'Yes. I mean no. Don't do that, I'll be out in a minute.'

She pulled the bath robe tighter around her, knotting

the tie firmly and took a deep breath. Unlocking the door, she stepped out into the bedroom.

He was perched on edge of the bed, his legs stretched out in front of him. He looked so... He looked like the man she'd always wanted. Jess's courage failed her.

'You're pregnant.'

She supposed that he could hardly fail to come to that conclusion from the amount of time she'd spent in the bathroom. Jess nodded her head.

'Hey. It's all right Jess. We're in this together and we're going to deal with this. I think we both need you to say it, though.'

The stress lines were back on his face. This was no walk in the park for him either.

'I'm pregnant. Seven weeks.'

He nodded. 'How do you feel?'

Jess swallowed hard. 'Fine. About the same as I did half an hour ago.' Apart from the fact that everything had changed.

His gaze had never left her face. 'Seven weeks. I guess its heart will just have started beating by now.'

'Yes. And its head is forming. Little bumps for its arms and legs.' Jess almost choked.

'Hey, there.' He was on his feet, holding her tight, before she even realised that she was shaking. 'I told you, we're in this together. I can provide whatever you need.' The words sounded hollow, almost like a business deal.

'I can look after myself.' However much it cost her, however alone she felt, she couldn't use this as an excuse to bind him to her.

'I know. I'll just tag along, then, while you're looking after yourself.' He smoothed a strand of hair out of her eyes. 'I can be your second-in-command. Hold your hair while you're being sick.'

'You will not.' She dug him in the ribs and heard his sharp intake of breath. 'I can hold my own hair, thank you very much. You can do the mopping up.'

He chuckled. 'That's the spirit. Look, let's give ourselves some time to let this sink in. What do you say I make some breakfast? Unless you *are* feeling sick again.'

She was feeling sick and terrified, exhilarated and somehow serene. 'No. I'm fine. And, yes, breakfast would be great.'

'Good.' He was halfway to the bedroom door and he stopped. 'Jess. You don't have to say anything, right now. But when you know...when you know what you're going to do...'

'I'm keeping my baby.' That was the one thing she was stone-cold certain about.

He nodded. 'Thank you.' He turned, as if he didn't want to show her what was on his face. Closed the bedroom door behind him, leaving her alone again.

Greg wiped the tears away. He was completely unprepared for this. When she'd said she was pregnant, all he'd wanted to do was to hold her. And although he had been torn by almost every emotion he could think of, when Jess had pulled herself up to her full height, faced him and with more than a trace of defiance in her eyes, had told him that she was going to keep her child—his child—his heart had almost burst with relief.

He would make things right. He could learn how to be a father. He could afford to give Jess and his child everything they might need or want. That he could promise right now. As to the rest—he was unclear about the scope and detail of that, but it was early days. He'd work it out as he went along.

His finger tapped on the kitchen counter as he waited

for the kettle to boil. Two beats for every one of his own heart, a little more maybe. He could almost feel that tiny heartbeat, racing away, powering the prodigious growth of a seven-week embryo.

He prepared breakfast, and was gratified to see that Jess ate all of hers. They took a walk in the park, talking about anything and everything. Everything but the thing that was so palpably on both their minds. Then lunch and he waited, with only a trace of impatience, for her to settle herself down to watch a film so that he could open his laptop and spend a couple of hours answering his emails.

Four hours later he found her asleep on the sofa, the DVD looping through the opening credits.

'Jess…Jess, honey, wake up.'

She opened her eyes, and smiled at him. Stretched, yawned behind her hand and then sat up. 'What's the time?'

'Nearly five. How are you doing?'

'Fine. You?'

'I'm good.' He sat down next to her on the sofa. Maybe he should have checked up on her, thought to cover her up while she slept. But the flat was warm and it seemed that all she needed right now was to get some rest. And what he needed to do was to take care of business. Make sure that he could provide for her.

She nodded. 'I suppose I should be getting back home.'

'Stay a while. Unless there's something you need to do.'

'No. There's nothing.' She shrugged. 'Well, nothing that can't wait. Today's been…'

'Yeah. Nothing much else matters, today, eh?'

'No.' Her gaze flipped to his laptop, closed now on the coffee table, where he'd dumped it when he'd come in here to find her. Then back to his face. 'Greg, I've been thinking.'

'Yeah? Not dreaming?'

She grinned. 'That as well. But before I fell asleep, I was thinking.'

Her cheeks were still flushed from sleep, her brown and gold eyes reflecting the light. Greg laid his finger against her lips, feeling the echoes from that one soft touch reverberate across his skin. 'Tell you what, why don't we have something to eat, and then I'll take you home. Let's make a time to talk next week, when we've both collected our thoughts.'

She twisted her mouth wryly. 'You mean you're making a plan.'

'Aren't you?'

She shrugged. 'Do I need a plan?'

'I think so. And you should take your time over it, decide what you really want.'

'That's easy. I want to have this child, look after it and love it the best I can. That's the only plan I need, isn't it?'

Perhaps it was. Perhaps he wasn't going to get a say in what happened from now on. 'I was thinking more about a plan for how I can help you do that.'

A flash of defiance. This wasn't going to be a walk in the park but, then, Greg hadn't expected it would be. 'Yes. Yeah, I'm sorry.'

'Don't be. However you feel is okay. Just don't stop talking to me, Jess.'

'No, I won't.'

'Good. That's all I ask.' Greg had a feeling that this was going to be much more complex, more daunting that he could imagine right now. He'd deal with the emotional side of it, he had to. For the time being he'd do his best to help her with the practical things.

He'd started to pace now. It was what he generally did when he had something to think through, but Jess wished he'd stop for a minute and come and hold her.

'I think you should speak to Gerry. He'll be able to give you the support you need work-wise.'

'I will. It's a bit awkward.'

'He's not an ogre, you know.'

'I know. But he's not just my boss, he's your best friend. I need to think carefully about what I'm going to say to him.'

'You're pregnant. You're not going to be working any more double shifts. What more is there to say?'

Jess couldn't look at him. She appreciated what he'd done today, supportive without being pushy, never once questioning that the child was his or that he shared a responsibility towards it. But he was unnerving her. All this sudden talk about shared decisions, practicalities. Her first, unthinking reaction was that she was going to be doing this all by herself.

'He knows about you and me. He's sure to put two and two together.'

'Just tell him, then. It's my child.' His Italian ancestry broke through his English reserve, his shoulders straightening and his proud head held high. For a moment Jess thought he was going to challenge her to a duel. 'You tell Gerry or I will. In fact, I've got a better idea, I'll meet you tomorrow and we'll go and tell him together.'

'We will not.' She wasn't going to put herself in that position. Taking each one of them on separately was challenging enough. Both at the same time was obvious insanity. 'I'll speak to Gerry.'

'If that's what you want.' A flash of that luminous, slightly wicked smile. 'I imagine he'll call me out for playing above my league.'

Jess snorted with laughter. Greg had a habit of taking the world and abruptly turning it upside down, making her feel that anything was possible. He didn't have a league, he was one of a kind.

'Right. Please tell me you weren't born that charming. I've suddenly got an interest in your genetic traits.'

'I wouldn't worry. I expect your genes are all dominant.'

She wrinkled her nose at him. 'I'll go and see Gerry tomorrow morning.'

'And I'll meet you at lunchtime.'

'Yeah. Only I might be a bit late.'

He sighed, as if he was dealing with a recalcitrant teenager. 'Not too late. You need to take your breaks.'

'Have it your own way.' His stubborn insistence on her welfare might be irritating, but she couldn't help liking it a little. 'And talking about food, I thought you promised me something to eat.'

'How does pasta e fagioli sound?'

'Just right. How do you make yours?'

He grinned. 'Nah. If I tell you…'

'I know. You'll have to shoot me, or challenge me to a duel.'

He nodded. 'And as I'm not going to follow through on either, I'm just going to have to keep my mouth shut.'

CHAPTER TWELVE

GREG HAD BEEN up since six, even though he wasn't due on shift until this afternoon. Partly because there was no point lying in bed when he couldn't sleep. And partly because tussling with the non-stop drip-drip-drip of emails into his inbox was about the only thing that made any sense at the moment.

His mobile rang and he punched the answer button irritably, without even looking to see who was calling. 'Yeah?'

'Good morning to you, too.' Gerry's voice sounded down the line, and Greg considered hanging up on him. Who knew whether Jess had seen him yet or what she'd said?

'What is it, Gerry?'

'First of all, try not to sound so grumpy when you answer your phone, it puts people off. Second, I hear congratulations are in order.'

'Thanks.'

Gerry paused, just in case Greg wanted to volunteer any more information. He didn't. He was in the middle of reading a report, and his eyes were still flipping back and forth across the words on the screen in front of him, although not much was registering.

'Greg!'

He'd lost the thread of the report's argument now anyway. Greg sighed and snapped his laptop shut. 'Yeah. Sorry, Gerry. I was in the middle of something there.'

Gerry snorted. 'Get used to it, mate. Babies are world champions for interrupting things.'

That was as may be. Gerry seemed to thrive on the loving, noisy chaos that seemed to erupt at his house at the unlikeliest of times. 'I can handle it.'

'I'm sure you can, and I wish you the very best of luck with it. Maura and I are always on hand for any parenting tips, though. Or you could borrow Jamie if you wanted a bit of practice. Actually, you can borrow him until he's eighteen if you feel that's of any help.'

'Keeping you up nights, is he?' Greg wondered whether he'd have the chance to roll out of bed and stumble to the nursery to hold his own child.

'Ah, not so bad.' Gerry chuckled. 'And even if this is as worry-free as both of you seem to be making out, I've still got a bottle of the good stuff in the cupboard if you decide you've got the time to pop in.'

'Thanks, mate. There was something I wanted to talk to you about, actually.' Greg knew he probably shouldn't be doing this but he did it anyway. 'Did Jess mention anything about her shifts to you? She looked pretty tired yesterday and if she's been working double shifts...'

Gerry laughed. 'Fussing already, eh? Pregnancy isn't an illness, you know.'

'I know.' Did it really sound as if he was fussing? 'Look, Gerry, I know I shouldn't ask, but I'd take it as a personal favour.'

'I don't do personal favours. All my staff get treated the same, and I'll be reviewing Jess's shifts with her this afternoon, just as I would with anyone else in her situation. Anyway, this is something you should be talking to Jess about, not me.'

'Yeah, I know.' Easier said than done. Greg looked at his watch and groaned. 'Listen, thanks for calling, but I've got to get going. Catch up with you later?'

'Sooner would be better.' Gerry's chuckle sounded in Greg's ear and then he cut the call.

Even though they'd made no solid plans to meet up, Greg had made sure that he caught up with Jess every day this week. Sometimes for a meal break, sometimes just for ten minutes snatched from a busy shift. He didn't need to, but Jess couldn't deny that she appreciated it, or that she looked forward to seeing him.

She hadn't seen him yet today, Fridays were always busy. That meant he would be looking for her, wouldn't it? That he would notice she was gone. Jess closed her eyes, wondering if that would make the darkness around her seem any less menacing, and pulled her cardigan around her. He would come. He'd find her.

Greg's phone rang and he ignored it. Gerry was going to have to wait, he had to concentrate on composing a particularly tricky email, and he only had fifteen more minutes left before his meal break was finished.

'There you are.'

Gerry's voice broke his train as he entered the room and Greg rolled his eyes. What did a man have to do to get some time to himself around here?

'What are you doing here?'

'Trying to get a bit of peace. I've got to get back to the London office before the end of today.' Greg sighed and snapped his laptop closed. It was about time he got back to work now anyway. This would have to wait until he got ten minutes for a coffee break.

'Have you seen Jess?'

'No. Why?' He supposed that Gerry had noticed that he was hanging around Cardiology rather more than usual and had divined that he'd been keeping an eye on her.

'Because she should have been back from her lunch break nearly an hour ago. Jess is never late.'

Suddenly the demands of the first and the second job shot into insignificance. 'Well, where is she? Didn't she say where she was going?'

'It's not my practice to get my team to tell me where they are for every waking moment.' Gerry's voice was calm, but Greg could hear the note of concern. 'Otherwise I'd have cottoned on to you a lot earlier than I did.'

'Yeah, right. Thanks for that, Gerry.' He had to think. Ignore the other things that constantly seemed to be crowding in on him and concentrate. 'Has she taken her coat?'

'No. She must be here somewhere, but I've paged her and called her mobile and she's not answering. Her sandwiches are still in the fridge.'

'Hmm. She wouldn't have gone far without them.' His groundless, lingering fear that Jess would simply not turn up for work one day, that she'd disappear along with his child, was looking less and less like an explanation for this. No one did a runner at lunchtime, leaving their coat and sandwiches behind. 'Do you think she's gone somewhere to put her feet up and fallen asleep?'

'I've checked all the common rooms and overnight accommodation. And the canteen. She's not down in A and E and she isn't in the admin offices. I had Beverly look in all of the ladies' lavatories and I've put a call out to all departments for her.' Gerry shrugged. 'I don't know where else to look.'

The knot in Greg's stomach was twisting tighter and tighter, as each possibility was ticked off an ever-diminishing list. 'Perhaps she's been kidnapped.'

'Leave off. This is a hospital, not a gangster movie.'

True enough. But Greg could—would—pay any sum to keep her safe. He wondered vaguely what safeguards his father had put into place on that score, and decided to shelve the matter until he got a chance to talk to Pat.

'Yeah. I just can't think. You don't suppose it's something to do with this history project she's doing on the hospital?'

'Maybe. She had a load of old photographs and was taking new ones for a "then and now" the other day.'

'Yeah, but she'd take her coat for that, wouldn't she?' Greg hoped with every fibre of his body that none of those old photographs had taken her into disused parts of the building. 'What about the basement? That's where the records are kept, right? She told me that there was an old safe down there…' For a brief moment Greg and Gerry stared at each other. Then Greg was on his feet and running for the stairs.

He almost stumbled on the steps down to the boiler room, and made the records room breathing hard. Pulling the door open, he called for her.

Nothing. In the far corner he could see a large metal door and he ran down the narrow corridor between the stacked boxes, dislodging one and letting it spill unheeded onto the floor behind him.

'Jess!' He tried to open the door and then beat on it with his fist. 'Jess are you in there?'

'Greg!' She sounded about a million miles away, but he could hear her.

'Are you all right?'

'Yes, I'm all right. Just locked in.'

'Sit tight, baby. I'll get you out of there.' Greg looked around for something that he could force the door with and saw nothing. In any case, he doubted whether the heavy security bolts would respond to a man's strength.

'Don't call me baby!' Her voice was faint, but he could hear the outrage in it and Greg smiled. It sounded as if she was holding it together in there. 'There's an air brick over the door. Can you see it?'

'Yes, hold on.' Greg fetched a set of steps, which leant against the wall, and climbed up, clearing the cobwebs from around the brick. 'Can you hear me better?'

'Yes. It's dark in here, Greg, the light's broken.' There was a plaintive note to her voice now.

'Just hang on. I'll send upstairs for the key.'

'The key's in here, with me, and there isn't another one. The door slammed shut behind me, and there isn't a key-hole on this side of the lock.'

Greg cursed under his breath. 'Okay. Can you reach the air brick? Don't try climbing on anything in the dark.'

There was a short pause, and the tips of her fingers appeared against one of the lower ventilation holes. 'Just about. But the key's too big to get it through.'

'That's all right. I can break a bigger hole out.' The old brick was crumbling, and it looked as if a well-placed shove would knock it out. 'Can you get back a bit? Be careful.' If she fell, and couldn't reach back up to the brick again, they'd be back where they started.

'Right.' He heard the sounds of her moving warily across the darkened room and then her voice again, fainter this time. 'Okay.'

'I'll be one minute.' Greg remembered he'd seen a se-lection of old tools abandoned in the corner of the boiler room. 'Then, when I give the word, I want you to cover your face.'

The brick was tougher than it looked. His first blow merely sent chips spinning back in his face, and Greg had to deliver two more before it gave and the chisel punched through to the other side. He called to Jess, and a minute later the key was slid through the hole and into his possession. Then she was in his arms.

'It's okay.' She was shaking, but Greg couldn't tell whether it was from the cold or from shock. His hand found hers. 'Are you all right? You're freezing.'

She nodded against his chest. 'I'm fine. Just a bit cold.' She seemed to be trying to burrow into his arms, and Greg held her tight, willing his own body heat to radiate into her.

'How long have you been down here?'

'I'm not sure. Since the beginning of my meal break.'

'That's almost two hours.' He rubbed her shoulders and back, trying to warm her, and she smiled up at him.

'That's better. I'm sorry.'

'What happened?'

'I came down here to get one last pile of documents for scanning. I wedged the door and put the key in my pocket.' She turned the edges of her mouth down. 'Fat lot of good that was. The admin staff made us promise to keep the key on us at all times, but neglected to mention that it was no good if we got locked in.'

Greg glanced down at the door wedge. 'Someone should have thrown that away years ago. It's not enough to hold a heavy door. Look, it's gone straight over the top of it.'

She didn't even glance downwards. 'Thanks. But it was my own stupid fault. I should have looked for myself.'

He wrapped his arms around her shoulders, settling her against him. That was where she was supposed to be. The place her body seemed to fit exactly. 'Accidents usually happen when we're not looking. That's the thing about them.' He ran his hand down her back, rubbing in the smooth, circular motion that he knew would calm her. 'Sure you're okay?'

'I'm fine.' She answered the question that he hadn't dared to ask. 'The baby's fine, too. She's used to the dark.'

'She?'

'Yeah. She told me.'

He chuckled. 'Must be right, then.' This was nice. For the first time in months everything seemed as it should be. The cold dread that had pushed every other worry out of his head had now given way to thankfulness that he'd found her, and it seemed to suffuse his whole body.

He dipped his head and planted a kiss on her brow. It really was the only thing that a man could do in the circumstances. She tipped her face upwards so he could reach her lips. It was impossible to do anything other than kiss her again.

She was always soft, always sweet. There was always that touch of fire that made his body react, as if his cells held the memory of her touch, craving it again. There was always more, too, and this time the sheer happiness of something averted curved her lips into a smile against his.

'Thanks, Greg. For coming for me.'

He'd been too busy to even notice that she had been missing. 'It was Gerry who told me you were gone.'

'You found me, though.'

She gave him too much credit. He could tell her so, or he could resolve to do better in future and move on. 'I'd better give him a call. Let him know that you're okay.'

She nodded. 'There's no phone reception in here. You have to go outside, into the corridor.'

He let her go, long enough for her to lock the secure room door again and gather up the pile of documents she'd come for. Greg considered confiscating the key so that she wouldn't be able to come down here again without him and decided that would be construed as over-protective.

The corridor outside, leading to the boiler room, was

a welcome few degrees warmer and he stopped, leaning against the wall and pulling her against him between his outstretched legs. Pulling out his phone and dialling Gerry, he curled his other arm around her waist.

'Gerry, panic over. I've found her.' He regretted the word '*panic*' as soon as the tips of her ears started to redden. 'I'm getting on to Maintenance—that door really isn't safe. It slammed shut even though Jess wedged it open.'

She looked up at him, a brief thrill of gratitude in her eyes. Greg imagined that she'd been sitting down here wondering whether she'd get a hard time for allowing herself to get locked in down.

'But she's okay?'

Thank you, Gerry. If he wasn't allowed to fuss, then perhaps he'd leave Gerry to do it for him. 'She says so.'

Gerry went for the bait. *'Well bring her up here. I want to make sure.'*

'Right.' He snapped the phone shut and grinned at Jess. 'Gerry wants you up in Cardiology.'

'I know. I've got things to do.'

'He wants to make sure you're all right.'

'I'm fine. I said so.'

'Hypothermia?' He pulled her closer to him.

'Somehow I don't think so. It wasn't that cold in there.'

'Shock?' Greg amended that to cover any possibility of imminent deterioration. 'Delayed shock. Delayed hypothermia perhaps. You've laddered your tights, so I imagine you've probably grazed your knee as well if I look a little closer.'

'Are you by any chance fishing for a diagnosis, Doctor? Because I have to tell you that making things up isn't going to work.' The glint in her eyes told Greg that she had his number. Fooling her was infinitely more difficult than fooling himself.

There was only one honest answer. He kissed her. He
was going to have to do better, keep a closer eye on her.
Unobtrusively, of course, or she'd call him out on it. He'd
think of a way, though.

Jess wasn't used to being looked after. She wasn't used to
the feeling of wanting to be looked after either. Greg had
delivered her up to Cardiology, where Gerry had taken
over as guardian-in-chief and had insisted that she sit for a
while and relax, while he saw the patients who were waiting for her. Then, at six o'clock, Greg had appeared again,
and despite all her protests he'd guided her into a waiting
taxi and taken her home.

'Don't you have something to do tonight?' He'd hung
around until she'd given in and asked him up for a cup
of tea.

'No.'

'Liar.' The quick dip of his gaze had betrayed the truth.

He shrugged. 'Okay, you got me. But if you want some
company… It won't do anyone any harm to wait on a decision from me for twenty-four hours.'

'Let them stew, you mean.' She grinned at him. Maybe
keeping Greg occupied tonight wasn't such a bad thing.
Every time she'd seen him this week he'd been disentan-
gling himself from one set of responsibilities so that he
could shoulder another.

'Yeah. I have a life too.'

'Glad to hear it.' And she needed him here. No, scrap
that, she wanted him here. Needing him felt as if she was
betraying her unborn child. She'd made a promise that
she would look after it and no one, not even Greg, was
going to put that into jeopardy by eating away at her in-
dependence now.

He looked around at her sitting room. 'This is nice. Cosy.'

'Small, you mean?'

'No. If I'd meant small, I would have said small.' He flopped down on the sofa. 'It could be bigger, though. Ever thought of expanding?'

Jess rolled her eyes. 'In which direction? There are flats above and below me and to either side. Guess I could build out over the pavement, but the planning authority might have something to say about that…'

He held his hands up. 'Okay. But if the people around you ever want to sell up…'

'They don't.'

'They might. Depends how much you offer them.' He had a look of exaggerated innocence on his face.

'Don't even think about it, Greg. There's plenty of room here for me.' She knew exactly what he was driving at. 'And the baby. For the time being, anyway.'

He nodded. 'Yeah. But you don't need to… What I mean is that you do have a choice, Jess. You can live wherever you want to. You could come and live with me.'

As invitations to move in went, this one was distinctly underwhelming. 'You want an answer to that?'

'Of course I do.'

A meal, a little candlelight and some kind of declaration of love would have been nice. He might just as well have emailed her. Or got the irreplaceable Pat to do it for him. 'I'll get us some tea, shall I?' It looked as if that talk that she'd rehearsed in front of the mirror and then with variations while she'd been trapped in the dark today was just about to be enacted for real.

CHAPTER THIRTEEN

SHE PULLED THE coffee table back to give him room to stretch his legs, and put a cup of herbal tea in front of him, sitting down at the far end of the sofa. Honey for sweetness. Biscuits, in case the need for calories threatened to make either of them cranky. Soothing lighting and a couple of candles in the fireplace, just in case Greg decided that their future together was a matter of romance, not business.

'So. You said you'd been thinking.' His eyes were dark, unreadable in the flickering light.

'I have. You want to hear it?'

'Always, Jess.'

Promising start. Now the difficult part. The only way that she could do this was to try to divorce herself from the heady feelings of love and the terrifying dread of loss that came with all of her dealings with Greg. 'This baby... You...' She took a deep breath. 'This is your child. I know that we took precautions...'

'Precautions fail, Jess. I never doubted for one minute that the child is mine.'

'Not even a minute?' They'd always used condoms. Sometimes a little hurried, their minds always on other things, but they'd been careful. Jess had thought they were being responsible.

'No. I won't say that I didn't think about it, but...' he

waved away any doubts that he may have had, as if they were nothing '…I trust you. There's no percentage failure rate on that.'

Warmth swelled in her chest, and Jess found herself smiling. 'Thank you. That's a really nice thing to say.' This was going better than she'd dared hope.

'So what else?' He leaned back on the sofa, as if he had all the time in the world. So different from usual. The way he might have been all the time if no one had thought to create Shaw Industries, or laptops, or email accounts.

She was trembling. The only way she knew how to do this was to pitch straight in. 'You have a right to a relationship with your child and I won't deny you that.'

'Okay.' A hint of suspicion crept across his face. 'Were you thinking about trying?'

'No!' She'd lost her way already in the maze of possibilities and emotions. 'Of course not. I didn't mean that at all. That's what I want too. I'm just trying to say that I won't ask anything from you that you don't want to give.'

'Understood.' He was obviously suspending judgement until he had the full story.

'And for Rosa and Ted, too. If they want an involvement… I mean, they have a right to a loving relationship with their grandchild. I'll do all I can to make sure that happens.' Jess could think about how she was going to accomplish that later.

He seemed to loosen up a little. 'Thanks. I think I can speak for them both in saying that they'll really welcome that. And that they'll really appreciate the fact that you thought to suggest it.'

'Well, those family recipes are too good to waste.' She grinned at him, trying to lighten the mood a bit.

Greg chuckled. 'Consider that done.'

'That's great.' They were getting somewhere.

'And how do you feel about me, then?'

His face was grave again. He'd picked up on the one thing that Jess couldn't make sense of, and asked the one question that she couldn't answer. Her imagination seemed only to stretch to two at a time. She and Greg. She and the baby. Three was a difficult and unmanageable number.

'How do *you* feel?'

He turned his dark gaze on her. As soft as silk and as demanding as any woman could ever want. 'I'll answer, even if you won't. This is my child too, and I want to be a proper father. I have the resources to give our child everything.'

What was that feeling of panic doing, quivering in her stomach? Wasn't that what every mother wanted to hear? 'I don't need your money, Greg. I've always provided for myself and nothing's changed. When I said that I'd welcome your involvement, I meant some of your time. Your love.' Maybe she'd gone a bit too far there. 'For the baby, I mean.'

'Not for you?' His eyes dared her to say yes.

'It's not me we're talking about here.'

He let out a sharp laugh of disbelief. 'What happened to being honest about how we feel, Jess? Are you going to tell me that you're sleeping with me but that you don't expect me to care about you? It's all just for kicks, is it?'

She couldn't break that faith. The trust that showed in his eyes and that she felt in her heart when he made love to her. 'You know it's more than that, Greg.' Of course he did. She could see it in his face right now. 'Although I don't discount the kicks. They're pretty good, too.'

'You've got a point. Why don't you come over here?'

'No. We're supposed to be talking.'

'You can talk from over here.' He was grinning now. Talking was about the last thing on his mind.

'I'll lose my thread.'

He gave a mock sigh. 'Yeah, me, too.' A pause, and then he hit her with it. 'Jess, I think we should think about getting married.'

'What?' She was already shrinking away from him when she realised that probably wasn't the thing any man wanted to see when he'd just proposed to a woman. If this could be construed as a proposal. 'Greg, you don't have to do that. '

'I want to.'

At this moment he probably did. He wanted to provide for his child. She should have expected this. Greg could be stubbornly honourable at times. But it was all far too risky. She'd known that there was always the possibility that things might not work out between the two of them, that his work schedule might swallow him up again, but she couldn't take that risk for her child. Marrying him now could just trap them both in a life of waiting for him.

She took a deep breath. 'I know you do. And I appreciate it, Greg, more than I can say. But I really don't think this is the best way forward.'

'Jess, this isn't just a business agreement.'

'I know, but my answer's still the same. It wouldn't be fair on you or me or our child. Let's find another way, eh?' She smiled at him. Tried to jolt him out of the rose-coloured, impractical world that he seemed to have steeped himself in.

An echo of the man she loved flitted across his features. The man who took what he wanted and gave so much in return. Then it died.

'Okay. We'll find another way.' His smile was carefully constructed. Proper in every way. 'I'll have to put you on notice that I won't be letting you turn all my offers down so easily, though. And I expect you to talk to me, Jess. You know that I can afford to give you whatever you want.'

Fair enough. There was something. 'I'll be having my first scan at sixteen weeks.' She hardly dared ask. Money was so easy for him to give but this might cost him far more.

'I'll be there. Just tell me when and where.'

'Thanks. I appreciate it.'

He reached out for her and she slid along the sofa towards him. The contact made her shiver both with warmth and foreboding. 'Don't say that. I want to see him just as much as you do.'

'Him?'

'Yeah. You reckon it's a girl and I think it's a boy. We could make a wager if you like.'

The look on his face told her that this was one bet she didn't want to have to pay up on. 'What kind of wager?'

'If I'm right then I get to keep you in my bed for a whole weekend. Somewhere nice. Paris maybe.'

'And if I'm right?' Jess was almost tempted. Who was she trying to kid? The temptation was pretty much unbearable.

'You get to keep me in yours for a whole weekend. Somewhere else nice. Rome perhaps. You'd like the house in Rome.'

She narrowed her eyes. 'Couldn't we just keep it simple? I bet you a fiver it's a girl.'

He sighed. 'I thought you weren't after my cash. Okay, a fiver it is. Or we could push the boat out and go for a tenner. You're missing out on a great opportunity, though. You really would love the house in Rome.'

'So you keep saying. Maybe another time.'

'I'll keep you to that.' His finger found her wrist, caressing the soft skin at the base of her palm. 'And what about tonight? Can I stay?'

'I'm…I'm tired, Greg.'

'I know. I just want to hold you.'

She wanted that too. Even if it did seem somehow dis-loyal to her baby.

He leaned forward, until his lips almost touched hers. 'We could keep it simple. Do whatever comes naturally.'

Jess gave up the unequal struggle. They'd covered enough ground tonight. Tomorrow was soon enough to tackle the rest.

Greg was like an addict. He said he'd give it up, had ac-tually managed to give it up for days on end when suffi-ciently threatened, but he always went back to it. When deprived of his laptop for more than a few hours he began to get jittery.

There was no end to it. Taking Friday evening and Sat-urday off had only piled on the pressure. The following week he seemed busier still and correspondingly more distant.

'Rosa called me last night.' Jess had cooked their eve-ning meal and was stacking the dishwasher.

'Hmm?' Greg didn't look up from his laptop.

'She said that she and Ted were leaving for Ecuador next week. They wanted to know if I'd like to go along.' Rosa had offered her congratulations and tremulously wondered whether it was too early to ask if anyone else was buy-ing her a pram. And if the answer to both questions was no, whether she might be allowed to take her out shop-ping for one.

'Hmm.'

'I said yes, that would be lovely.'

'Good.'

'She seemed pleased.' Rosa had been delighted.

Greg looked up and focussed in Jess's direction. 'Good.'

'You think it's a good idea, then?'

He looked at her, suspicion flickering in his eyes. 'Am I missing something?'

Jess got to her feet. 'Yeah. You're missing something. Do you want a cup of tea?'

He nodded. 'Love one. You're such a star, Jess.'

'Jess, are you free? I've got a friend of yours down here.'

Greg's voice on the phone sounded relaxed, as if he was smiling.

He was still smiling when she got to A and E. 'What's up?'

He jerked his head towards one of the cubicles. 'Thomas Judd. You know him?'

Jess couldn't place the name. Greg grinned. 'Ten years old, fair hair and a very cheeky smile. When I examined him I found he has a pacemaker and he said that he'd had it replaced about six months ago.'

'Ah, yes, Tommy. Is he all right?'

Greg nodded. 'Yep. Involved in a car accident. Minor cuts and bruises and I've had the technician down to give him a pacemaker check to make sure that none of the wires were dislodged by the impact.'

'Where is he?' Jess scanned the cubicles. 'I'd like to go and see him.'

Greg caught her arm. 'His mother's here too. She's pretty knocked about but she'll be all right.'

Jess nodded. Her first road accident in A and E had reduced her to tears, until Greg had taken her to one side, explained that this was one of those cases that looked a great deal worse than it was and had sent her back in to clean and stitch the cuts on the man's face.

'She doesn't want Tommy to see her?'

'No. His father's on the way. '

'I'll go and sit with him. I've got time, I'm just about

to take my lunch break.' A warning frown clouded Greg's brow and Jess ignored it.

He opened his mouth and then thought better of it. Greg knew as well as Jess did that if he objected to her working through her lunch break he wouldn't have a leg to stand on. 'Okay. Just for half an hour.'

Tommy wriggled free of the nurse who was cleaning his cuts and hugged Jess when he saw her. 'I'm very glad you're here.' He enunciated the words as if he were a spymaster, about to send Jess out on an important mission.

'Well, I'm glad to be here. What's up, Tommy?' The boy was unusually uncooperative, batting away the nurse who was trying to tend to him. He'd already seen far too much of the inside of a hospital in his short life, and this level of treatment was something that he usually took in his stride.

'Get off me!' Tommy was clearly having nothing more to do with the nurse who was gently trying to tend to him. She winked at Jess and backed off.

'All right.' Jess sat down by the bed. 'You can tell me what's the matter and then I'll finish with those cuts. Deal?'

'Deal. Only I want you to do something first.'

'What's that?'

'Go and look after my mum.' Tears sprang to Tommy's eyes. The kid who was so brave, hardly ever cried. Jess choked back the lump that had suddenly formed in her throat.

'Tommy, she's got another doctor looking after her. He's much better than—'

'I want you!' Tommy thumped the bed. 'You have to go!'

'What's all this?' Jess hadn't been aware that Greg had entered the cubicle, and when his voice rang out behind her, it made her jump.

'I want Jess to see my mum. She's the best doctor in the hospital.' Tommy explained the situation slowly to Greg, just in case he was having trouble comprehending.

'Tommy, I'm not—'

'Good idea.' Greg cut her short. 'But first Jess needs to see you, so she can tell your mum that you're all right. And that you're doing what you're told.' Greg folded his arms, a sign that he wasn't having any nonsense. 'All right, chief?'

Tommy nodded wordlessly.

'So when Jess gets back she'll expect to see that cut on your forehead with a dressing on it. Which means that you need to keep still for Erica while she does it for you.' Kindness had been vying with firmness from the very start, and Greg was clearly having trouble maintaining his authoritarian stance in the face of Tommy's blue eyes. 'I'll bring you something to drink when I get back. What would you like? Some juice?'

'It doesn't matter. Just water.' Tommy was interested in one thing only, and everything else was unimportant.

'All right. But first of all I'll take Jess to see your mum.'

Greg closed the cubicle door behind them. 'Bright kid. Knows how to work the system.'

'He ought to, he's had enough practice.' Jess shrugged. 'He's not usually this awkward, though.'

Greg chuckled. 'I'd do exactly the same in his place. If one of my family was sick or injured, I'd do whatever I had to do to get them the best treatment I could.'

'Is it okay if I pop in to see his mother?'

'What, you were thinking of going back in there and trying to pretend you'd seen his mother when you hadn't?' Greg gave a snort of laughter. 'Good luck with that one.'

It looked as if Tommy's mother had broken her jaw. Major swelling, contusions and bruising. No wonder no one had thought it a good idea to let Tommy in to see her.

Jess smiled at the nurse tending her, and the nurse took the opportunity of someone else being there to slip out for five minutes.

Gemma was lying on her side so that blood and saliva could drain from her mouth, and recognition flared in her eyes as soon as Jess sat down next to the bed. 'I'm one of Tommy's doctors from Cardiology. I've just seen him and he's fine and being well looked after, but he's worried about you. So I promised him I'd come to see you and find out how you were doing.'

Gemma's gaze never left Jess's face, and Jess took hold of her hand.

'Don't try to talk, Gemma. Give me one squeeze for yes and two for no. Do you want your phone?'

One squeeze. Jess hadn't really needed to ask. She'd seen Tommy's face when he'd got the messages from his mother, telling him that she was there for him. Jess reached for Gemma's bag and found her phone, fumbling with it for a moment before she found what looked like the correct application, and held the screen up in front of Gemma.

A smile for Tommy, drawn with his mother's finger. A bit shakier than the ones that he used to receive when he was in hospital but that didn't matter.

'Here, you send it.' Jess saved the image into a text and found Tommy's name on the contacts list. His mother stabbed her finger on the 'send' button, and the time bar flashed up then indicated that the message had been sent.

'There. He'll be getting that right about now. I'm going to go back tell him to look on his phone.' Just in case the nursing staff had found Tommy's phone and managed to persuade him to switch it off.

Gemma's hand found hers and squeezed it.

'Hang on in there, Gemma. Your husband will be here soon.' For the life of her Jess couldn't remember Gemma's husband's name, but Gemma was bound to know who she meant.

Another squeeze.

'Is there anything else I can get you?'

Gemma's finger pointed towards Jess and then her thumb jerked towards the door.

'You want me out of here and go to see Tommy?'

Gemma patted her hand then squeezed it once.

'Okay. I'll come back and see you again. In the meantime, just hang in there. I've spoken to the doctor who's looking after you and you're going to be okay.'

Gemma's eyes filled with tears and Jess dabbed at them with a tissue. Her thumb jerked again, towards the door.

'Okay, I'm going.' Jess's eyes misted with tears. She knew that Gemma would rather be with strangers if it meant that Tommy had a friend with him. She would do the same for her own child. Suddenly she wanted more than almost anything to go and find Greg, to tell him.

A quick thumb's-up from Gemma and Jess turned and made for the door, scanning the space outside for Greg. A rattle from the bed behind her made her turn. Gemma's arm was flailing back and forth in a repeating arc, banging against the bed rail.

'Greg. In here,' she called to him, and out of the corner of her eye she saw him turn. She didn't need to question whether he'd come or not, and she ducked back inside the cubicle.

Gemma's eyelids were fluttering and she was groaning. Jess hurried over to her, checking quickly that her breathing was unobstructed.

She felt, rather than saw, Greg enter the cubicle. 'She's having a seizure.'

'Okay.' Greg was at Gemma's side, steadying her gently

so that a sudden movement wouldn't pitch her off the bed. 'How long?'

'Thirty seconds. A minute tops.'

The motion of Gemma's hand began to slow. 'Good. She's coming out of it now.' He bent over her. 'Okay, Gemma. You're all right. Try to relax.'

Gemma was slowly coming back. Greg was there, and however much it pained her to leave, Jess had somewhere else to be. 'Do you need me any more?'

'No, I think we're good.' Greg was smiling at Gemma, his hand reassuringly on her shoulder. 'Could you ask Steve to come in here, though? And if you see the husband when he arrives, find out if there's any history of seizures…'

He looked up from Gemma for a moment and their eyes connected. Just for a moment, but that was all it needed. After weeks of feeling that Greg was slipping away from her, that even when he was right there with her he was somewhere else, suddenly he was here. They were together.

'Anything else?'

'Go and check on Tommy.' He was grinning.

'Yeah.'

'Get me a cup of tea?'

'Sorry didn't quite catch that one.' She heard his exclamation of mock dismay as she turned on her heel and didn't need to look back to know that he was smiling.

CHAPTER FOURTEEN

IT WAS COLD up here. Jess wrapped her hands around her mug of tea.

'This is…' Greg shrugged. 'I don't really know how to describe it.'

'No, me neither.'

'Let's have a look at that photograph again.'

She handed him the scanned copy of the photograph that she'd found, and Greg studied it. 'So this window, here…' he ran his finger across the image '…is that one over there. And if I stand here… Yes, this is where the photo was taken from.'

Jess went to stand beside him. 'I think you're right.'

He looked around him. 'So this was a ward once. Right up here in the attic.'

She nodded. 'Yep. They used it for cholera patients during one of the outbreaks in London.' Jess shivered. The whitewashed walls, now lined with store cupboards, must have seen their share of suffering.

'Do you know the date of this photo?'

'Yes, it was written on the back—1851.'

Greg was deep in thought. 'Before Lister's procedures were adopted.' He shook his head. 'These doctors didn't even know that they needed to wash their hands. All they could do for infectious disease was put the patients up here. It must have been terrifying.'

'They did the best they could.' Jess looked for the hundredth time at the faces of the doctors and nurses, posing for the camera in well-ordered lines. 'We wouldn't be here now if it wasn't for them.'

'No.' Greg sat down on a large, wooden crate, leaving space for Jess to come and sit next to him. His face was drawn into a mask of regret, and he seemed to need her close.

'I didn't think it would be this sad. I knew the facts and figures, how there were so many things then that couldn't be cured, but when I see the faces…'

'Yeah.' Greg put his arm around her shoulders. 'See that kid in the bed there? Look at his arm, it's so thin.'

'Mmm. He can't be much older than Tommy. How's Gemma, by the way?'

'She's okay. They've wired her jaw and are keeping her in under observation. There have been no more seizures, though, and the CAT scan didn't show any reason for concern.'

'Good. Is that where you were just now?' Greg had said that he'd meet her half an hour after the end of his shift.

'Yes. I met her husband up on the ward. Nice guy.'

'And how's Tommy?' Jess knew Greg. He wouldn't have left without finding that out as well.

'Good. Texting his mother smiles, the way that she did when he was in hospital.' He grinned. 'So you can cheer up.'

Jess laughed. 'Right. Consider me officially cheery. Do you have time for dinner tonight?'

'Yes. In fact, there's something I want to tell you.'

'What?'

'I'll tell you when we eat.'

Jess searched in her handbag and found a couple of fruit bars. 'Here.' She handed Greg one and stripped the other of its wrapper. 'We're eating now.'

He laughed. 'I bet none of your Christmas presents last until Christmas Day, do they?'

She shrugged. 'Some of them do. But tell me now.' Their time together was too precious to waste. Dinner was about the only opportunity they got to just talk about nothing. Be together, without the distractions that seemed to press relentlessly in on them.

'I've made a decision.'

That sounded serious. Maybe she should have waited. On the other hand, they were alone here. 'Yes? What decision?'

'I can't keep on doing two jobs like this. Something's got to go.'

Thank you. At last he'd come to his senses. The cutting back on his hours at the hospital hadn't worked, Greg was just as busy, just as tired as he'd been when he'd been working a full shift rota.

'I think you're right. You can't keep this up for much longer.'

He nodded. 'So I've decided to leave the hospital. Run Shaw Industries full time.'

She could almost hear the silence. Almost feel the seconds, painfully ticking by. She mustn't do all the things she wanted to do—rage at him, cry and beg him not to do this. Greg wouldn't listen. He was driven by the practical. She had to be calm. 'This... Are you sure, Greg?'

'Sure's a luxury that even I can't afford.'

There was some hope, then. 'Perhaps you should think about it a little more. Not do anything hasty.'

'I have to make a choice. You yourself said that I can't

go on like this. I'm not doing either of my jobs to the best of my ability.'

'But you love medicine. This is what you studied for. Everything you've worked for. You can't just give it up.'

'There are other doctors.'

'Not as good as you.'

He curled his arm around her shoulders. 'Thanks for the vote of confidence. But there *are* other doctors, and the hospital will fill the vacancy easily. I'm the only one who can keep Shaw Industries going.'

'They've managed without you all these years.' Jess hated that damned company. Wished it would crumble into dust.

'That was when my father was alive. Jess, he's left me this responsibility. I can't not shoulder it.'

Why not? There wasn't any point in asking him. It was his father's first and last gesture of confidence in Greg, and he could pass that up about as easily as he could wave a magic wand and cure all ills. He might be good, but he wasn't that good.

'I know it's not what you expected, Jess. But this is the way forward. I can provide for you and the child.'

'Don't use me as an excuse for doing this. If you needed to provide for us, you could do it on a doctor's salary. And you don't. I can provide for myself and the baby. We've been through all this already.' She glared at him.

A muscle at the side of his face twitched. 'I'm not. But it's a fact, Jess. Like it or not, I'm in a position to be able to provide for my family.'

And try stopping him. Greg's mind was obviously made up on this point, and arguing about it with him would get her nowhere.

'The baby needs your time, too.'

'And this doesn't facilitate that? I've just cut my work commitments in half.'

But it was the wrong half. Couldn't he see that?

'The baby needs you.' She couldn't explain it. She'd clung on to the hope that Greg could be a better father than his own had been. Wondered if maybe, over time, he could show her how being in a family with him might work. Now she was beginning to doubt it.

He sighed, pinching the bridge of his nose as if he had a headache. 'Jess, you're making this complicated. I'm not telling you where you ought to work or what you should do. Shaw Industries isn't just a faceless, evil conglomerate, you know.'

'I dare say it isn't.' Jess frowned. That was how it appeared to her, and she was going to need a fair bit of convincing to think any other way.

'Do you know what we do?'

'Engineering?' Something like that. Jess hadn't taken a great deal of notice.

'Yeah, design and engineering. It started out when my father invented a drill head—which doesn't sound very exciting, but it was ground-breaking in a number of different areas. The basic design has applications of all sorts, it's even used downstairs in the operating theatre here.' He looked at her steadily. 'It might not be as much of a medical breakthrough as Lister made, but every little helps.'

He had an answer for everything. Everything apart from what would happen to his soul if he was separated from the job he loved, the one he'd chosen, and started to trudge in the treacly footsteps of his father.

'Is this really what you want to do, Greg?'

'It's what I have to do. At some point you have to choose whether what you want is more important than where you can do the most good. It's not about being happy, it's about doing the right thing.'

It sounded like a life sentence. A life behind bars, for something he hadn't done. Jess could think of nothing more to say to him. She was going to have to wave him goodbye and think about baking a cake with a file in it. Trouble was, Greg didn't seem to want to escape.

'This'll be okay, Jess. We can make this work. Let me show you.'

'How are you going to do that?'

He slid his hands around her waist. 'This weekend. I'll pick you up at seven o' clock on Friday night. Bring a toothbrush.'

'Sounds interesting.' Greg was trying to charm her out of all her reservations. He wasn't doing a bad job of it either. 'Where are we going?'

'Do you need to know?'

'Yeah, I do.' However much Jess was tempted to plunge into the exciting unknown with Greg, it still frightened her. It should frighten her. She had responsibilities now, and the tried and tested was always going to be preferable to the heady gamble that Greg offered. 'I need to know where I'm going.'

He nodded. 'Okay. We're going to Rome.' He quieted her protests with a finger across her lips. 'You don't have to do anything, it's all arranged. I've got to go over there to see the new headquarters building on Saturday. I'm hoping we'll have Sunday to ourselves.'

'I don't know, Greg.' It sounded fabulous, but it wasn't exactly the kind of thing that Jess did. 'Italy for the weekend?'

'Is just the thing. We'll stay at the house in Rome. You'll love—'

'Yes, I know. I'll love the house in Rome.' She should

at least try to see his point of view, for everyone's sake. And seeing Rome with Greg didn't sound like too much of a hardship. 'I'll be able to make my own mind up about that at the weekend, won't I?'

Something ignited, deep in those dark brown eyes. He pulled her close, wrapping his arms around her shoulders. 'Good. Thanks, Jess. I know things haven't been great recently. I've been under a lot of pressure, and things have been complicated. Thanks for sticking by me.'

'Isn't that my line?' She snuggled into him. She never got tired of his scent.

He chuckled. 'Not really. You have all you need, Jess.'

It didn't actually feel as if she was anywhere different. Since the car had picked her up at her flat, Jess had been shepherded through two airports at top speed and with the minimum of fuss, having had a good meal and a nap on the plane. She wasn't sorry that she hadn't had to struggle with airport officials and taxi drivers, or get lost in a foreign city, or study each coin as she counted it out of her purse. Somehow, though, in the absence of these inconveniences the house in Rome might just as well have been in any city in Europe.

They arrived in darkness. No chance to stop and see where she was as Greg caught her arm and hurried her inside. As he opened the front door, the car they'd come in slid away into the darkness. Jess imagined it would be back tomorrow to take them wherever they wanted to go. Greg opened the front door and picked up their weekend bags, ushering her inside.

She'd been half expecting an Italian version of the Victorian monstrosity he'd taken her to on their last weekend away. Nothing could have been further from the truth. Warm, clean lines that drew you in, past the graceful curved staircase, towards a kitchen that was stylish but also comfortable and unmistakeably designed for home cooking. A sitting room that didn't just invite you to sit but demanded that you take your shoes off, make yourself at home and join in the conversation.

'Rosa chose this house, didn't she?' The house bore none of the hallmarks of Greg's father's taste and all of the characteristics of his mother's.

'Yes. Is it that obvious?'

'Yup.'

He looked around. 'Yes, I suppose it is. Mum came over and chose the house and decorated it for him about ten years ago.'

'So she never lived here?'

'No. When she comes home she goes to Milan to be with her family.' He caught Jess's look and laughed. 'I told you their relationship was complicated. They were always friends, even though they were divorced. In fact, I think their relationship worked better when they weren't married.'

'Fewer expectations?'

'Yeah, I guess so. He wasn't much good at being a father or a husband. Once you accepted that and stopped expecting him to be home for things like Christmas and birthdays, things got a great deal easier.'

Jess swallowed hard. All her fears encapsulated in one damning sentence. But Greg was different. Wasn't he?

'So do you like it?' When Jess didn't reply, he nudged her. 'The house. Do you like it?'

'It's beautiful. Stunning, actually.'

He nodded, clearly pleased. 'Thought you would. Want to see upstairs?' The curve of his mouth was enough to chase everything else away for the moment.

'Yes. Are you going to give me the in-depth tour?'

He flashed her an I-don't-know-what-you-mean look. 'Bathroom probably. Hallway…inevitably. Bedroom.'

'Just one?'

'Just the one that matters.'

'Which one's that?' She reached forward, running her finger up the buttons on his shirt until she got to the top one.

'The one that has a box on the bed. Gift-wrapped.'

'Gift-wrapped?'

'Yeah.' His hands slid to her hips, pulling her against him. 'I like a bit of gift-wrapping.'

The nightdress lay spilled on the carpet where he'd tossed it in a heap of lace and silk. Jess had never had anything so luxurious and had loved the way it had felt on her body. Loved even more the way it had felt when he'd slowly peeled it off. Since they'd found out about the pregnancy, their lovemaking had changed. It had become more tender and sensual. As if all the things that they couldn't say might be encapsulated in a caress. Jess sighed. There were quite a lot of things that they couldn't, or wouldn't, say at the moment.

He was still asleep, and when she shook him he growled and rolled over. Fair enough. How he managed to function on the amount of sleep he'd had in the last few weeks was a mystery to Jess anyway. She poked him in the ribs and he protested groggily.

'I'm getting up. Just going to have a look around. I won't go far. Be back in an hour.'

'Uh. Okay.'

'You stay here.' He didn't answer and Jess supposed he'd gone back to sleep. Just in case, she wrote him a note and propped it up on the nightstand.

The house wasn't the largest in the small square but it

was the prettiest. Not ostentatious but oozing quiet class. Jess put the key that Greg had left in the hallway into her pocket, and looped the strap of her handbag across her body.

It was cool, but not as cold as London, and Jess left her gloves in her coat pocket. She looked around to get her bearings and fix the position of the house in her mind before she started out. Five minutes took her out of the quiet, sleepy streets and onto the main road.

Suddenly she knew she wasn't in London. The sound of Italian, spoken in the street. Different smells, different sounds. A teeming city, so like her own and yet so different.

'Breakfast.' Jess grinned to herself. 'I'll go for breakfast.'

She found a café. It was too cold to sit on the pavement but there was a seat by the window, where she could watch the world go by. The waiter's English and her Italian were more than enough to get her what she wanted from the menu.

She'd been to Italy before, when she'd been a student. Had slept on the train, her head on her rucksack, and shared a small cottage with three friends, far enough from anywhere to be affordable. This might just as well be another country, it was so different.

'Ciao, bella.' A man sat down opposite her at her table and Jess looked around. There were plenty of free tables.

All the same, he seemed intent on conversation. Jess couldn't understand much of what he was saying but his general drift was pretty obvious. She wondered whether a polite but firm rebuff would be better delivered in her shaky Italian or in English.

'Scusi...' A young, fair-haired man, dressed in a dark jacket and jeans, was towering over them both. 'The lady's with me.' He smiled amiably at the man opposite Jess, who gave a shrug and left.

'Who are you?' Now this second man had sat down at her table. At least he spoke English, so it was going to be more straightforward to send him packing.

He'd already reached into his jacket and pulled out a wallet, opening it to display an ID. The photo was unmistakeably of him and the card bore the logo of Shaw Industries. 'Joe Callaghan, ma'am. Security.'

Jess scanned the card and raised her eyebrows. 'Senior Security Officer, no less.' She leaned across the table towards him and whispered, 'So Shaw Industries is interested in the security of this café? What is it? A drop point for industrial secrets?'

'Nothing so exciting. Our only interest in this place is that currently you happen to be sitting in it.' Joe seemed quite unflappable. So far, anyway.

'So if I go somewhere else...' There really wasn't any point in asking, she knew the answer to that one. 'Have you been following me all the way from London?'

'No, I work for the Italian branch of Shaw Industries. My wife worked for the British Embassy over here and when we started a family we decided to stay.'

Nice touch. 'Which might lead me to believe that you're a trustworthy kind of fellow?'

Joe laughed. 'It appears that Mr Shaw thought so.'

'Dr Shaw? Or his father?'

'The younger Mr Shaw. He doesn't use his title in the company.'

Jess swallowed. It felt like Greg's last betrayal of all that she'd thought he held dear. But that wasn't Joe's fault. 'So when did you start following me around?'

'You make it sound like surveillance. I'm just here for your safety. There's a big difference.' There was a hint of steel in Joe's easygoing smile. 'And I've been here since last night.'

The thought that Joe might have been in the house somewhere occurred to Jess and she reddened. Catch-me-if-you-can, naked in the hallway, suddenly didn't seem as good an idea as it had in the small hours of that morning. 'Where *did* you spend the night last night?'

'In the guest house.'

'The flat over the top of the garage? With the red door?' Which just happened to be completely self-contained.

'That's the one.'

'And what? You were just looking out of the window and saw me walking past. So you decided to follow…protect…me.'

Joe gave his slow, easy smile. 'No. The security system alerts us when anyone goes in or out of the main house. And it's not up to me to decide anything. My instructions are to look after you.'

'Your instructions from whom? Dr Shaw?' Shaw Industries might call him Mr but she wasn't Shaw Industries. 'Did he know you'd be looking after me?'

She must have betrayed her indignity. The nagging thought that Greg had let her wander off on her own a little too easily this morning. Joe smoothly went into maximum tact alert. 'I get my instructions from Mr Shaw's personal assistant.'

Pat again. Jess wrinkled her nose. 'What's she like? Pat?'

'I've never met her. She seems very nice on the phone.'

'I'm putting you in a difficult position, aren't I?'

Joe suppressed a smile. 'Nah. A different position maybe. My job is to blend in with the furniture, not make conversation.'

'But it won't make much difference if you have coffee with me?'

Humour flashed in his face. 'Yeah, it'll make a difference. I won't be wishing that you'd waited until I'd had breakfast before you left the house.'

'Operation Coffee it is, then.'

Joe rolled his eyes and motioned to the waiter. 'Just coffee will do fine.'

CHAPTER FIFTEEN

JESS OPENED THE front door, fully aware that Joe had paused and was waiting to see her safely inside. Greg was still in bed, but he stirred when she walked into the bedroom.

'Hey, there. Enjoy your stroll?'

'Yes.' She climbed onto the bed and sat astride his body. 'Guess what happened?'

'What?'

'I got saved by Joe from Security.'

A flash of uncertainty appeared in his dark eyes. 'Saved from what?'

'A man sat down at my table while I was having coffee. Spoke to me in Italian.'

'Oh. Really?'

Jess nodded gravely. 'Really. It was terrifying. Good thing that Joe was there to rush to my rescue.'

He was man enough to know when he was beaten. 'Fair enough. I dare say you could have dealt with that on your own.'

'I dare say I could.' Gripping his wrists, Jess leaned forward, pinning his arms against the pillows. He grinned, stretching beneath her and tipping her forward slightly.

'Joe's been teaching you a few moves, eh?'

'No, this one's all mine. And just for the record, Joe

was a model of tact. Didn't even admit that it was you who had me followed.'

'Protected.'

'Whatever. I doubt you could have done any better your-self.'

'Clearly not. Are you going to let me up?'

'Not until you tell me why you thought it was a good idea to have me tailed by your security team. And how long this has been going on for.'

'Joe was called in last night. There wasn't anyone up till then.'

Jess sat up straight, letting him go. 'What were you thinking, Greg? That I can't manage for myself outside London?'

'It's nothing to do with that, Jess. I know you can look after yourself, but I can't help it if I want to do that too.'

'You're being over-protective.'

He sat up, wrapping his arms around her, and she slid into his lap. 'Maybe I am but I don't care. I'd do anything to keep you and the baby safe, Jess. When you got locked in that vault and we couldn't find you...'

'Right. You're not going to let me forget that, are you?'

He sighed. 'Why should you? I can't.'

'You can't be with me every minute of the day, Greg.'

'I know. And I've got to get going soon.' He kissed her. 'So Joe will make sure you've got everything you need today.'

She was in Rome. There was so much to see, so much to do, and she wanted to do it with Greg. Wanted him to show her this beautiful city. Jess swallowed her disappoint-ment. 'You have to go?'

'Yeah. Sorry, sweetheart, but I did tell you that this was a working visit.'

Yes, he'd told her. And Jess was beginning to understand that all the excuses she'd been making to herself were just that. Work came first. First, last and apparently most things in between.

'Mmm. When do you think you'll be back?' She hated the tone that crept into her voice every time she asked that question. Needy. Wheedling.

Greg rolled out of bed and padded towards the bathroom. 'I'm hoping to get this over quickly but I may be late. It depends.'

There wasn't much point in asking what it depended on. When Greg said that he might be late, there was no need to wait up. 'I'll go and do some sightseeing, then, and you can always call me if you finish early. Is it all right for me to ask Joe if he'll show me around?' She followed him into the bathroom, watching as he stepped into the shower.

'Of course.'

'He's not going to be busy with…whatever he does?'

Greg laughed, turning in the shower. 'Going where you go *is* what he does for the next couple of days. I'm sure he'll find it far more interesting to give you the grand tour than sit around all day.'

She'd hoped that Greg would find it more interesting to give her the grand tour than sitting around in a meeting all day. The thought seemed to stick in the back of her throat as the muscles there knotted into a lump and instinctively she swallowed.

'Oh, and, by the way, he has a company credit card.'

'Meaning?'

He laughed, leaning out of the shower to kiss her. A few drops of water fell onto her sweater and Jess brushed them away. 'Meaning that if you want to go shopping, he'll use it to pay the bill.'

* * *

'So how was your weekend?' Reena caught Jess on her way to the canteen on Monday morning.

'Great. I had a lovely time. I've got some grappa for you in my locker.' Courtesy of Shaw Industries. Joe had persisted in pulling out the company credit card at every opportunity, and finally she'd let him choose a couple of bottles for her to bring home with her.

'Fabulous. Thanks.' Reena took her arm and leaned a little closer. 'What I really want is the goss.'

'Sorry.' None that Reena needed to hear or that Jess wanted to tell her. If she didn't think about it, maybe it would go away.

'You just spent a weekend with Greg in one of the romance capitals of the world. Don't give me sorry. Give me something more substantial.'

Right. Well, she'd spent both days with Joe, after Greg had been unable to get away on Sunday either. They'd walked for miles and seen some of the sights, but that probably wasn't what Reena wanted to hear. And Jess wasn't about to go into details about her nights.

'We saw the Trevi fountain.' If she didn't elaborate on the *we* then that sounded just the kind of thing that Reena wanted to hear. It was actually just the kind of thing that Jess wanted to be able to say.

'Yeah? That's so-o-o romantic. Did you throw a coin in?'

'Of course I did. What do you take me for?'

Joe had told her to turn her back and throw the coin over her shoulder. And when Jess had been a little too eager and thrown too high, the coin had hit something, bounced back and skittered across the paving stones until Joe had trapped it under his foot. He'd said that hitting the water on her second try was enough to ensure her return to Rome, but Jess wasn't so sure about that.

'Sounds great.'

'It was. We had a lovely time.' Just not the one her heart had wanted. She'd rather have been locked in the sluice room for the weekend with Greg. The thought made her smile. They could save that till next weekend maybe.

'So how was yours?' Best change the subject now, while she'd merely given the wrong impression, rather than telling any actual lies.

'Oh, fine. Good, actually. I got a lot done. I've finished all of the costumes for the carol singers.'

'Yeah? That must have taken you a while.'

Reena shrugged. 'It wasn't as difficult as we'd thought. Is that all now?'

'Well, we've got the model, the costumes, the carol sheets and enough books for the storytellers.' Jess counted everything off on her fingers. 'I've printed out all the documents and photos to go with the model and sorted out the rota for the ward visits. So, not counting any last-minute emergencies, I think we're all done.'

'With two weeks to spare.' Reena thought for a moment. 'Is that making you as nervous as it does me?'

'Yes. Feels all wrong, doesn't it?'

'Mmm. We should do it all now, before anything has a chance to go pear-shaped. Anything can happen in between now and Christmas.'

Jess squeezed Reena's arm. 'Nothing's going to happen. We're just not used to being ready in such good time.'

'That was down to you. If you hadn't started planning all this in August, we'd be running around in ever-decreasing circles and ever-increasing panic.'

Jess grinned. At least someone seemed to notice what

she did. 'Hang tight. Nothing's going to happen between now and Christmas. You'll see.'

'Have you got some time tonight?'

Jess looked at him as if it was a trick question. 'Yes. Why? What's up?'

'Shaw Industries has just vaporised. I've got a spare evening.' Greg had meant it as a joke but was surprised to find that a part of him rather liked the idea. Jess obviously approved of it as well.

'In that case, is there anything particular you want to do?'

'Actually, there is. I'll meet you in the canteen after I finish my shift.'

They rode together through the dark streets, the windows of the taxi streaked with freezing rain.

'You like this, don't you?' She tipped her face up towards his.

'Like what?'

'Rushing me off somewhere without telling me where we're going or what we're doing.'

'I like surprising you.' The line felt like...it felt like just a line. Something to say to keep the peace and prompt a smile.

'You mean you like a fait accompli.' She grinned up at him. 'If you don't tell me where we're going then I don't have a chance to object.'

She had a point. 'You mean I'm afraid of what you might say?'

'Are you?'

'Terrified. You scare the living daylights out of me.'

She bumped her shoulder against his and laughed. Funny, that. The way he was in absolute earnest and yet it didn't even occur to Jess to believe him.

He made the taxi stop at the entrance to a mews so that he could walk with her on his arm, down the dark, deserted street. She could look around, get an idea of what the place was like.

'You like this?'

She shrugged, looking around her. 'Very nice.'

Maybe she'd like it a little better when she knew what they were doing there. Greg withdrew the estate agent's key from his pocket and located the front door that he wanted.

She was watching him gravely now. 'What's going on?'

'This property's for sale. I wanted you to take a look at it.'

'You're thinking of moving?'

Greg didn't reply. All he needed to do was to get her inside and then maybe she'd fall in love with the place, the way that the blurb on the property had promised.

The rooms were surprisingly large inside the mews cottage. Jess imagined that in the daytime they'd be light as well. The furniture had been cleared and the walls were painted white, as if to give prospective buyers a blank canvas for their own imaginations. It was an amazing place. She couldn't think why he would want to move when his current location seemed to fit his needs so well, but as he obviously did, this looked like a place where he could be happy.

'There's a good school just around the corner.'

'Bit of a long way from my place.' An alarm bell began to clatter quietly in the back of her head. Like next door's smoke detectors going off.

'I was thinking that this could be your place. If you wanted.'

If only. 'I don't know, Greg. We said we'd leave that

decision for a while. Not rush things, just because I'm pregnant.'

'I'm not moving. This place is just for you.'

Jess looked around. Swallowed hard. The house was lovely. More than enough space for her and her baby. A little walled garden at the back and shops just down the road. 'Greg it's lovely, but...'

'If you don't like this one, my estate agent tells me that there's plenty of choice.'

'I imagine there is. How much is this cottage on the market for?' Jess couldn't make a stab at an exact sum but she knew it must be a lot. Probably more than she wanted to hear.

He shrugged. 'I can afford it. The only thing that matters is whether you like it or not.'

Jess could feel tears. Dammit, she wasn't going to cry. Tears would only give Greg the impression that she was labouring under a surfeit of happiness and that really wasn't the case. 'It's a lovely thought, Greg, and I do appreciate it, really I do. But I'm happy where I am.'

'I know. But you could be happier here.' He looked around. 'Or if you weren't, at least you'd have a bit more room to be as happy as you were before.'

'I can't afford to run this place, Greg. This is a private mews, there must be some kind of charge for upkeep. And the shops...'

'What's wrong with the shops?'

'Well, they're great, but they're all speciality shops. The kind of place I go into once in a blue moon. They're far too expensive for me to use all the time.' Jess stopped. She knew she was sounding ungrateful. But these were the kinds of practicalities that she had to think about. Babies didn't come cheap, and she was going to have to watch her budget.

'I thought of that.' Greg sat down on a pretty little window seat that looked out onto the garden and pulled an envelope from the inside pocket of his jacket. 'Here.'

'What's this?' Jess almost didn't take it. She really didn't like the look of it.

'It's a formal offer. I want to support you and the baby, and I want that support to be legally yours. If anything happens to me, I don't want anyone to be able to take it away from you.'

'Greg.' If he had been trying to make her feel miserable and embarrassed, he couldn't have done a better job.

'Look, Jess, I heard what you said about being independent. I understand that you don't want our relationship to affect our child. This means that it doesn't. It gives you a place to live and an income, no strings attached. It's a good place to start from.'

'Greg, no.' This was all too much. He'd sprung it on her so quickly and she couldn't think straight.

'Just read it. It gives you a much better income than you have now and is index-linked. There's provision for school fees, a college fund and a small trust fund for our child. A place to live—here if you want or wherever else you choose.'

He could do this. He could buy her, and her child, so easily. 'And what about the things I said I really wanted, Greg? What about your time? Your love? A father to go to for advice when our child needs it? Are they itemised in here too?'

He shook his head slowly. 'You can't make those things part of a contract, Jess.'

'Right. Absolutely right.' She proffered the envelope back towards him and he didn't move to take it so she laid it on the window seat, next to where he was sitting.

'Jess, I know that I've been busy recently.' His face was

stony now. She was alone in the house with a complete stranger. 'But things will be different. Everything will settle down in time.'

That was another piece of advice that her mother had drummed into her. Never go into marriage thinking that you can change a man, because it won't happen. Her mother had learned that the hard way with her father. This wasn't marriage, it was a contract. One that would bind her, and her child, to him. 'I don't want this, Greg.'

'You mean you don't want me.'

How could he think that? 'I mean that I don't want my life, my child's life, to be spent waiting for you. However much you can provide in a material sense, if you can't be there, it means nothing.' Tears began to trickle down her face. She was being inflexible, she knew that. But clinging to what was familiar was all she knew how to do right now. It had been her mother and herself, just the two of them. She had the blueprint right there.

'Jess, you're being impractical. What's wrong with accepting an easier life?'

'That's it, though. It's not an easier life, or a better one.'

'And what is? Living in a flat that's too small, counting the pennies? If that makes you feel virtuous, fine. But I'm not going to let you limit my child's opportunities.' There was no anger in his voice. Just a flat assertiveness that was colder and crueller than any emotion.

'Not going to *let* me? Greg, listen to what you're saying, please. My flat is perfectly adequate for me and the baby. You can't make me move.'

'No?'

This was how he did business, then. Jess supposed that he'd learned this kind of attitude in the boardroom. He'd become used to getting whatever he wanted.

'Just try it.' She turned on her heel and made for the front door. Behind her she could hear his footsteps.

'Jess.' His hand appeared over her shoulder, holding the door shut. 'Look, I didn't mean that. But think about this. It's all very well to be independent, to be able to fend for yourself if you have to, but this is crazy. I have a right to give my child a decent place to live. You can't just throw that back at me and tell me that you're all right on your own.'

She turned to face him, her back pressed against the door. 'You're wrong, Greg. You think that spending money is going to absolve you of every other responsibility. Well, it doesn't. My child can't be bought. That's non-negotiable, and if you want me to sign something then you can put that in your contract.'

'Ah. So all of a sudden it's *your* child. I don't have to be a doctor to know that you didn't manage to conceive it all on your own.'

She'd had enough of this. She'd tried not to be angry and resentful, but these days rage seemed to be simmering beneath the surface most of the time. And now it had broken free, like some living, breathing being.

'You don't need to be a doctor at all, do you? You're determined to throw away your career for the sake of Shaw Industries. What else are you going to throw away? Me? Our child? You're not going to get that opportunity, Greg. I'm not going to let you tie me up with contracts and agreements so that I lose who I am. Because who I am is all I have to give to my child.'

'You think it's so easy.' He almost spat the words at her.

'No. I think it's hard. You're the one who's taking the easy way out, and that's your prerogative. But don't expect me to just fall into line and support you in it any more, because I can't. I don't want it for you, or for me, or for the baby. That's the end of it.'

They stared at each other. The lines had been drawn and there was no going back now. He was too like his father. She was too like her mother. It had never had the faintest chance of working, they'd just been beguiled by friendship and great sex.

'Let go of the door, Greg.'

'I'll take you home.'

'The door.'

'Okay, then, I'll call a taxi.'

'I can find my own way home. Let go of the door.' Jess had to get out of there. Couldn't bear to look at him and see everything that she'd lost. He looked the same, but inside he was so very different.

He let go of the door and she pulled it open, almost stumbling out of it. She didn't hear it close behind her, but she didn't hear his footsteps either. She was alone, all the way to the high street, and then every step of the way home.

CHAPTER SIXTEEN

HE HAD TO find some kind of viable solution to this. It was obvious that things weren't going to work between Jess and him, she'd flung everything he'd offered her right back in his face. They'd have to come to some sort of agreement, though, for the baby's sake.

'This is it, then, Jess.' He had been talking to her all evening as if she was there, trying to reason with her. He knew that she wasn't going to budge and neither was he. 'This is the end of it.'

He re-read the email he'd written to his solicitor. If he and Jess couldn't work things out between them, he'd pay for someone to advise and represent her, and it would be a matter for the lawyers to negotiate. It wasn't the way he'd wanted it, but it looked as if wanting and getting were two entirely different things these days.

The cursor hovered over the 'send' button. This was the only way forward. No regrets and no more conversations with her when there was nothing here but empty air.

'Goodbye, my love.'

He clicked 'send' and his laptop responded with a tone, signifying that his email was on its way. Greg flopped back onto the sofa. In the morning he'd wake up and realise that he'd done the right thing.

A Future Christmas...

It was like a waking dream. Greg's heart was still beat-ing hard, as if he had fought his way out of some cloying danger, which he couldn't remember but which still clung to him, like a broken cobweb.

It was Christmas Eve. He was walking across the fields to his mother's house, the warm glow of the windows beck-oning him home. Outside a horse-drawn carriage clattered past on its way into the village, and when Greg looked through the front window of Rosa's house it seemed per-fectly natural to find a scene that looked like something from a Christmas card—a blazing fire, a Christmas tree and four figures dressed in Victorian costume.

Jess sat by the fire, talking to his mother. A little to one side Ted sat in a chair, watching a boy of about three play with a hoop and stick. Greg noticed, with some surprise, that Ted seemed to have acquired a set of side whiskers, along with his frock coat and starched collar.

He focussed on Jess's face. Pink cheeks in the firelight, small hands folded in her lap. A sudden jolt of longing transfixed him to the spot, leaving him helpless and beg-ging for some release from this. He had no idea whether Jess would respond to him differently in her new guise, but he didn't care. Just to touch the elaborate folds of her dress. To hear the silk rustle as she moved.

This wasn't right. He was just dreaming. He'd read the slim volume that Jess had given him from the library, and this was the kind of thing that happened when fiction combined with fact in the unconscious mind. Greg had heard about cognitive dreaming, and wondered whether he could change things, make them a little more realistic.

With an effort of will the picture merged and morphed into something different. Jess, in front of the fire, dressed this time in jeans and a warm sweater. She looked tired, the way any mother of a young child would. But where was his child? Greg craned against the window to catch sight of him.

He wasn't there. For the first time Greg realised that he was freezing cold, his silk business suit doing nothing to keep out the snow and the biting wind. All the same, he had to try and find his son. Working his way around to the kitchen window, he peered in.

He was there, with his grandmother, helping to make mince pies. Covered in flour, he was laboriously fashioning pastry circles with a plastic cutter. Greg found himself grinning. The boy had something of himself about him, dark hair and olive skin. But his face was that of an angel. Jess's face. Large hazel eyes that seemed to effortlessly combine intelligence and mischief. The way he laid his work out so neatly, his tongue trapped between his lips in concentration. He was just like his mother.

Ted appeared at the back door, stamping the snow from his wellingtons and throwing off his coat. The boy ran to him and he swung him into the air. Then Jess, at the kitchen doorway, smiling, happy. Or at least that was the way it seemed. By some preternatural sense that the dream afforded him, Greg knew that the smile was just for show, and that the single tear she brushed from her cheek wasn't one of happiness.

Greg was starving, freezing, right outside the window, but no one seemed to notice. He tried to tap on the pane but his arms were suddenly heavy. Looking down, he saw wide metal cuffs, soldered tightly around his wrists. Chains binding him.

He had to get them to see him. Had to make them know that he was home at last. He knew that Jess would welcome him. He could sit by the fire with her and warm himself.

Watch the light from the flames sparkle on the baubles on the tree. He would give everything he had in exchange for just five minutes, to hold her and his son and tell them both that he loved them.

The need was so great that it felt like a living, breathing thing. Greg made a lunge for the window, but found himself dragged backwards. Something was pulling him, back across the fields. However hard he tried to struggle, however much he instructed his sleeping mind to change the course of the dream, he couldn't. He fell, and felt the frozen ground, sharp against his face. Rolling over, he managed to get a glimpse of where he was being carried to so inexorably.

The glittering, ice-cold, steel and glass of the City were growing closer and closer. Looming over him, blocking out everything else. Greg tried to look back towards the old farmhouse, which currently housed everything that he cared about. But he couldn't.

Twisting, fighting with his bonds, roaring with frustration, he started to fall.

Greg landed on the polished wooden floor, banging his head on the coffee table on the way down. There was something digging in his ribs and on closer inspection it turned out to be his laptop. He cursed, disentangled himself from the power cable and looked at the clock on the mantelpiece.

Five minutes past midnight. He still had work to do but somehow he couldn't bring himself to be bothered tonight. How long had he been asleep? It seemed like hours, but the music CD he'd put on a while ago was still playing quietly in the background. Greg stood up and stretched. Maybe an early night would do him good. He was still half-asleep anyway, caught in the world of that crystal-clear dream. Tomorrow things would seem different.

CHAPTER SEVENTEEN

'HAPPY CHRISTMA-A-A-S!'

'Happy Christmas.' Jess smiled down at the little girl in the reindeer costume, trying to catch some of the child's excitement for herself.

'Ah, Jess. I've been looking for you.' Gerry caught his daughter's hand.

'Hi, Gerry. Are you all right?'

'I'm supposed to be a ghost, right?' He lowered his voice. 'I'm assuming that means deathly pale.'

'Well, the make-up's great. Just be careful you don't get carted off to A and E.'

'You think I overdid it, then?'

'Just a little. Do you think that people like to see their doctors looking worse than they feel?'

'In my experience most people don't notice. But perhaps I'd better go and wash some of it off. Will you keep an eye on Emma for me?'

'Yes, of course.' There wasn't much else to do. All of the volunteers had turned up and were getting on with their allotted tasks. Which was a shame, really. Something approaching a crisis might have taken Jess's mind off what seemed like a vast, empty void of today and tomorrow.

It was her own fault. She'd turned down every invitation for Christmas Eve and Christmas Day on the basis that she'd be somewhere else. Just as long as her friends and family didn't get together and realise that she hadn't been with any of them, she'd be okay.

'Unca Greg's going to be Father Christmas.'

'What's that, sweetie?'

'Father Christmas. With presents.' Emma was clearly shocked that Jess didn't know about Father Christmas.

'Ah, that Father Christmas. You mean the one who squeezes down your chimney every year to bring you presents?'

Emma nodded. 'Look, there he is.' She pointed over Jess's right shoulder

'But he's not here yet. He won't come until you put your stocking out tonight.'

'No.' Emma rolled her eyes. 'He's here.'

'Well, perhaps he's just taken the reindeer out for a bit of a run before their big night.'

Jess turned, her gaze following the line of Emma's pointing arm. Just as expected, Father Christmas wasn't standing behind her. But Greg was.

She let go of Emma's hood and the little girl flew into his arms. Greg hoisted her high and Emma squealed with laughter.

The only man she wanted. A laughing child in his arms. Here at the hospital, one of the 'Christmas Volunteer' badges pinned to his red sweater. Having to look at everything she'd lost, right there in front of her, was making Jess feel sick.

'Jess.'

Her name on his lips was all she wanted to hear, and everything she couldn't bear to. Jess scanned the corridor, praying that Gerry would return soon.

'Jess.' He tried again. This time his voice was quieter. More tender.

'Greg. Hello.' She focussed wildly on the volunteer's badge. 'You've come to help. Thanks.'

He grinned. 'It's an excuse.'

She imagined it was. This wasn't Greg's world any more and the only way that he would be here was if he had an ulterior motive. 'Even if it is, we'll put you to work. I'll take help wherever I can get it.' She felt herself redden. It had probably been the wrong thing to say to Greg on almost every level that she could think of.

He didn't take the advantage that she'd handed him on a plate. 'I wanted to see you, Jess.'

'I got the letter from your solicitor. I've done as he suggested and contacted one of the people on his list.'

'That's not what I'm here about.'

'There's nothing more to say.' She saw Gerry approaching out of the corner of her eye and Greg turned to follow the line of her gaze.

'Gerry. Mate, you look awful.' He grinned, handing Emma back to her father. 'Sure I can't…?'

'Don't you start.' Gerry shot him a baleful look and Emma squealed with happiness. 'Since neither of you seem to appreciate my ghastly visage, I'll take my daughter to see Father Christmas.'

'Unca Greg?' Emma beat on her father's shoulder excitedly.

'No, darling. We're going to see the real one.' Gerry glared at them both, took Emma's hand and walked away.

'He's going in the wrong direction.' Jess couldn't bear another moment of this. Not when Greg looked so much like the man that she had first kissed last Christmas and so little like the one he'd become in the intervening year.

'He'll work it out. Jess, wait, please.' He laid his hand on her arm.

'I can't, Greg.' If she stayed any longer she was going to start crying. She'd done enough of that in the last two weeks.

'You can.' He moved closer. Close enough for her to catch his scent. Indefinable, but it was his alone.

'This is all in the hands of the lawyers now. We're probably not even allowed to be talking to one another.'

'We can do as we please. And, anyway, I'm not sure that lawyers are the right way to go any more. I've changed my…agenda.'

'No.' If only he had. Her own heart wanted to believe that he had, but the tiny heart beating inside her? That was to be protected at any cost.

'I want you to come with me.'

'Where to?' Dammit, he'd hooked her in. She wasn't going to go with him so it didn't much matter.

'Just take the step. Come with me.'

'When I don't know where you're going?'

'Yep.'

'No, Greg. I can't.'

'It's Christmas Eve, Jess. Don't you believe in the magic?'

She sighed. 'What is this, a fairy story? You think that just because it's Christmas everything's going to turn out okay.' She turned, flicking her finger against one of the gold bells on the Christmas Tree. 'See? Nothing. It doesn't even ring.'

'Maybe you just can't hear it.'

Jess rolled her eyes. 'And maybe you're having aural hallucinations. Anyway, your timing's way out. It's not even Christmas Day yet.'

He raised one eyebrow. 'The first step is believing. If we believe…'

'I believe, Greg. But I believe in reality, not an idealised view of the world. Things don't just go away because you refuse to recognise them.'

'I meant if you believe that things can change then you can find a way to change them. If you don't come with me now, I will be back.'

Jess was under no illusions on that score. But she knew that whatever Greg's intentions were, he wasn't going to be able to keep them up for long. The company would drag him away. It would always drag him away, and no one could just click their fingers and make it disappear.

'That's up to you. Don't expect my answer to be any different.'

He nodded. 'Okay. See you, Jess.' He turned and walked away. Stood aside as someone negotiated a wheelchair through the wide doors into the reception area and then strode out into the square outside the hospital.

He'd given up so easily. Another trait that Jess didn't recognise. He'd be leaving after Christmas, and then he'd have other things on his mind. She couldn't compete with Shaw Industries, and she didn't have the energy to try.

She turned, blind to everything other than misery and the certain knowledge that she'd done the right thing. She cannoned into the Christmas tree and stumbled back again in a cloud of sparkly dust.

'Hey… Careful!' Gerry was on his way back through Reception, Emma perched on his shoulders. 'You okay?'

'Eh? Yes, of course.' Jess decided that Emma would probably be easier to fool than Gerry. 'Did you see Father Christmas, sweetie?'

'No. Daddy can't find him.'

'Really? Where do you think he is, then?'

'That way.' Emma pointed in the opposite direction from which they'd just come. 'But he was here.'

'Here? I didn't see him.'

Emma leaned forward and brushed her hand across Jess's hair. 'He made you sparkly.'

Gerry shrugged. 'You can't argue with that. Do you want to come and see if we can track the man down?'

'He's in the little sitting room next to the canteen. Follow the signs for the grotto.'

'A grotto! D'you hear that, Em? Shall we see if we can find it?'

Jess leaned over the basin in the ladies' room and tried to shake some of the sparkle out of her hair. She guessed it didn't matter too much, it was Christmas after all, but if she was going to go to any of the wards, it probably wasn't a good idea to go shedding bits from the Christmas tree everywhere.

Last Christmas everything had been so easy. It had been easy to believe in Greg, easy to work with him, easy to kiss him. He'd taken her on journeys that she'd thought were hopeless, defied the flat line on the monitor and kept working. The old Greg had taught her that you didn't stop while there was still some thread of life, some chance that a heart would start to beat again.

There was no chance. She had to be realistic. If she didn't let this go now, there would only be further pain and disappointment, which would drive yet another wedge between them. She couldn't risk that, for the sake of her child.

The look he had given her just now. That old, challenging look that defied the odds and had, on more than one occasion, saved someone. Jess's heart beat a little faster. In the mirror she could see her reflection, a hint of his defiance in her eyes. Then, hardly aware of having made a decision, she turned and ran for the door.

The courtyard outside the main entrance was full of people, but the one person she wanted to see wasn't there. She searched the faces desperately and then she saw him. Standing by a parked taxi, chatting to the driver.

'Greg!' She hollered at the top of her voice and began to run towards him. He turned on the instant and when he saw her he smiled.

'You haven't brought your coat.'

Jess realised that she was shivering in the crisp, morning air. 'No. I'll go back and get it.'

'No, you won't.' He took his leather jacket off and draped it around her shoulders. 'Get in.'

The driver already seemed to know where to go, cutting through back roads and emerging again onto the main streets, which were decked with lights and heaving with last-minute shoppers.

'Let me take that.' She still had her clipboard clutched to her chest and he tugged at it. She relinquished it with as much grace as she could manage and he slipped it into the carrier bag that lay next to him on the seat.

'It's not going to make any difference, Greg.'

'We'll see.'

'I'm coming because you asked me to. But things aren't going to change, you've made your decisions.'

He nodded. 'And you've made yours?'

'Yes. I've made mine.' Jess glanced at the sliding window between them and the driver and saw that it was firmly shut. They had some measure of privacy, probably up to about the level of a quiet sneeze. She'd keep her voice down.

'And that's not going to change. You won't consider moving out of your comfort zone.'

She opened her mouth to tell him that wasn't fair, and

then decided that it probably was. 'I'm out of my comfort zone now.'

He grinned. 'Yeah, me too. And that's exactly where we both need to be.'

CHAPTER EIGHTEEN

THE TAXI SPED across the river and turned up towards the City then bumped into a quiet cul-de-sac. They drew to a halt outside a three-storey building, separated from the road by railings and a neat portico over a solid, black-painted door.

Greg caught up his bag, got out of the taxi and paid the driver. Waited for Jess to follow and then took the steps up to the doorway in one stride, pulling the old-style bell handle.

Jess jumped when the door was opened almost immediately. No time to focus on the engraved brass plate at the side of the door. A young woman, who seemed to know Greg, stood to one side.

They might just as well have stepped back two hundred years. Polished dark wood doors, a huge, gilt mirror and a pair of high backed wooden chairs, next to a small Regency table with magazines displayed neatly on it. It was a waiting area, but clearly one that people didn't spend much time waiting around in. Just enough to phone upstairs, and for someone to hurry down to meet a valued client.

'Thanks, Sarah.' Greg gave her a smile. 'Is he in?'

'He's waiting for you in his office. Would you like to go straight up?' Sarah smiled at Greg and then Jess, the same well-regulated smile. 'Can I take your coat?'

'Thanks.' Jess handed Greg's coat to her.

'Shall I bring up some coffee?'

Greg nodded. 'That would be nice, thank you.' He reached into his bag and pulled out a parcel, which was obviously a well-wrapped bottle, proffering it to her. 'Happy Christmas.'

Sarah's veneer slipped a little and she blushed. 'That's very nice of you...'

'We won't keep you too long. I'm sure you've got better things to do today.'

'There's plenty of time. We always stay open until lunchtime on Christmas Eve.' Sarah disappeared with Greg's coat and left them alone to climb the long staircase, which curved up through the centre of the building. It was almost dizzying, drawing the eye upwards to the ever-decreasing circles above her head.

'I love this staircase.' He leaned close, as if that was some kind of secret. 'Apparently it's one of only a few in London that are quite this shape.'

'Yes. It's lovely.' Jess had given up now. No more questions, no more *let's get this over with*. It would all play out, and then Greg would go home and she'd go back to the hospital.

He chuckled, placing his hand lightly on her back and steering her across the first floor landing to an open door, where a middle aged man in impeccable pinstripes stood.

'Charles.'

'Greg.' The man extended his hand. 'How are you?'

'Well, thank you. I appreciate you being here today. Jess, this is Charles Hamlin. Of Hamlin, Grey and...'

'Hamlin.' Charles chuckled as if this was a very old joke that still somehow managed to tickle him. He held his hand out to her and she grasped it shakily. 'Dr Saunders. A pleasure to meet you.'

'Jess, please. Nice to meet you too.'

'Sit down, please.' He waved her towards one of two chairs that were set in front of a large slab of mahogany piled high with papers, strewn with various knick-knacks and lit by a reading lamp with a green shade.

Jess looked around at the book-lined office. Charles was a lawyer of some sort. Anger spurted through her veins and she almost turned and ran, back down the aristocratic staircase and into the street, where she might be able to breathe again. She felt Greg's hand again, light on her back. Stay. Please stay.

She should get out of there right now, but somehow she couldn't. Maybe it was because Greg seemed so different, so much like the man he'd once been. The man she'd follow into any darkness, through any unknown door, because she trusted him.

She drew herself up as straight as she could, pretended that she wasn't wearing jeans and a sweatshirt with sparkle all over it, and sat down. She crossed her legs tightly, and wished that Greg would give her back the clipboard so she could either shield herself or hit him with it, whichever turned out to be appropriate. At that moment Sarah appeared behind them with coffee, on what looked suspiciously like a silver tray. What *had* she got herself into?

Greg had placed another bottle-shaped parcel from his bag on Charles' desk, and he unwrapped it while Sarah was pouring the coffee. His smile turned into a beam of approbation as he examined the bottle. 'I say. Thank you, I shall enjoy that immensely.'

Greg grinned and Jess shot him a pleading look. If he didn't get down to business by the time she'd finished her coffee, and maybe one or two of those rather nice-looking biscuits, she was going to lose her nerve and she'd be out of there.

'I don't want to keep you. Perhaps we can start over coffee.' Greg seemed to sense that she was getting restive.

'Of course. Dr Saunders…Jess…I assume that Mr Shaw has explained why we're here this morning?'

'Actually, no. I'm in the dark at the moment.' She glanced at Greg, hoping he'd get the message.

Greg chuckled. 'That's my fault. Jess, Charles was not only my father's legal advisor for many years, he was also his friend.' He paused and Charles beamed across his desk at both of them. 'My father didn't discuss his business with me, or my mother, but Charles was one of his closest confidants. That's why I want you to hear this from him.'

'This is about your father?'

'It's about everyone. Trust me.' Greg waited for her nod and then settled back in his chair, gesturing to Charles that the floor was his now.

'John Shaw was an extraordinary man. He was bold, inventive and had an enormous, if slightly unconventional talent for business.' Charles spread his fingers in front of him on an empty area of the desk. 'I think that John would forgive me for saying that sometimes that talent didn't extend to his personal relationships. I knew him well, and liked him very much, but trying to gauge his personal feelings was often a very…shall we say…hit and miss affair.'

'You mean he could be distant.' There was no sense in beating about the bush. Jess had nothing to lose here, and it was beginning to look as if she had nothing to gain.

'Exactly. Which was why Greg needed my help.'

Jess pressed her lips together. If Greg wanted to fall in line with everything that his father wanted, that was up to him but she wouldn't endorse that.

'Don't you want to know why this has suddenly become an issue?' Greg was frowning at her now. Perhaps she should at least appear to show some interest.

'Um, yes. I was wondering that, but I didn't want to interrupt.'

Charles's gaze flipped quickly between her and Greg, perhaps wondering whether they were about to start squabbling between themselves. A moment of silence appeared to convince him that it was safe to go on.

'To cut a long story short, Greg has used a management model that his father explored but never implemented, which proposed a radical reorganisation of Shaw Industries. The power base of the company would no longer be one man but is vested in the board of a charitable trust. The company is run by the trust and the profits that would have normally gone to the CEO are used for charitable purposes.'

'And this was his father's plan all along?'

'No, it was just one of a number of feasibility studies. But, as in everything else, he was very thorough. This particular structure was designed along one of the principles of quality management.' Charles leaned forward slightly. 'No man is indispensable.'

Greg was indispensable to her. And this…the thought that he might not be to the company…was a glimmer of hope. 'In business terms, you mean.'

'Of course. I realise your own profession takes no heed of that aphorism.' Charles chuckled. 'In fact, I rather hope that every man is indispensable as soon as he enters your door.'

Charles was wandering again. This time it was almost charming. 'But Greg's father never did anything about those plans.'

'No. He gave me no reason, but he did ask me to store the papers safely.'

'And the plan would still work?'

'Absolutely. The paperwork was all drawn up and Greg

and I have been reviewing it exhaustively for the last week.' Charles's gaze flipped momentarily towards Greg.

'Yeah, exhaustively. And Charles has been advising me, exhaustively, about the personal financial suicide involved in making the changes that I've proposed.'

'Quite. But my duty is to facilitate.' Charles turned back to Jess, his expression softening. 'I imagine you're wondering why we're having this conversation here, instead of over a nice lunch and a glass of Chablis.'

'Um. Yes.' Jess hadn't been wondering that at all. She had been too busy wondering about everything else.

Charles laid a small bundle of documents in front of her. 'It will take some time to effect the change, but these documents will set the ball rolling, to some extent irreversibly. We agreed on them yesterday, and met again early this morning to proof the copies for signature. Greg wants to sign them now, but before he does so he has asked me to explain their implications to you.'

'I still don't understand.' Jess turned to Greg, not Charles. She wasn't interested in any finagling over the structure of Shaw Industries, she was interested in Greg's motivations. Whether he could make different decisions from those his father had.

He was grinning. 'The crux of it is, Jess, is that I want out. But I want the company to survive, because a lot of good people would lose their livelihoods without it. So I had to do the one thing that experience had taught me was only going to be a disappointment and try one last time to get to know my father.'

That she almost dared to understand. Hardly dared to believe. 'And...what? You deciphered the book he left you?'

He shook his head. 'No. But its existence made me re-alise something. My father gave the better part of his life to Shaw Industries, and he knew far better than I do how to keep it strong. If I wanted to leave the company able to survive on its own, I had to make my peace with the past and go looking for him.'

'And you found him?' Perhaps she shouldn't ask that question in front of Charles. Jess didn't care. It was far too important and she wanted to know now.

'Yeah. Inasmuch as I ever will. This is his basic plan, with a few tweaks that…' he grinned in Charles's direction and Charles ignored him '…sever my connection with the company completely. And with it my income from the company.'

'Which will, of course, affect both Greg's lifestyle and potentially that of any of his dependants.' Charles cut to the quick and softened the blow with a vague wave of his hand. 'But that's something that you should talk about privately. Will you excuse me?'

He was already halfway towards the door. 'Charles. Thank you.' Jess couldn't just let him go like that.

'It's my pleasure.'

'What do you think?'

Charles's gaze slid towards Greg again. Perhaps she shouldn't have asked. Greg was his client, not her.

A small nod from Greg seemed to assure him that an answer was in order. 'I think…' He seemed to be searching for the right words. 'I think that life affords us few opportunities of this nature. You should choose wisely.'

The door clicked shut behind him and for a moment Jess's gaze was caught in Greg's. Staring, just staring at each other, as if the next tick of the clock was too valuable to just squander.

'I'm glad you took the step, Jess. Thank you.'

'I couldn't do anything else. Is this really what you want to do, Greg? Sign away the company?'

'Don't you think it's a good idea?'

'I think it's the best idea you've ever had. You were meant to be a doctor.'

'Yeah, I know. I nearly made the worst decision of my life and let Shaw Industries eat me up just because I thought that it would finally bring me closer to my father. But even giving up the job I love wasn't enough to make me see.'

'What did make you see?' Jess was shaking. Please, please. Let it be what she wanted to hear.

'You and the baby. I can't give you up, Jess, not for anything. Certainly not for my father's company.'

It was as if someone had flung the windows open wide. Light and sound and happiness burst into the dark place that Jess had begun to feel that she was going to be living in for ever.

'I...' She swallowed. She had to be sure. However much it cost her, she couldn't just take her own happiness and leave the people who relied on Shaw Industries stranded. 'The company will be okay, though? In good hands?'

'Yes. My father's plan was a good one, and it included sizeable benefits for him. I get nothing—in fact, some of my own assets are being transferred to the company.' He grinned. 'I haven't much use for a racehorse. Or a private jet. And most of the houses will be sold, although I'm planning to keep the house in Rome.'

Jess grinned. 'That's a good choice. I do like the house in Rome.'

'I know, that's why I want to keep it. But, seriously, Jess, this is going to affect you as well as me. It means that I won't be able to give...'

She leaned forward and laid her finger across his lips. 'There's only one thing I want. And I'm making this request on behalf of me and our child.'

He smiled. Pure happiness seemed to radiate from him, warming the room. 'Anything.'

'We want you to be the man that you want to be, whatever that is. We want you to give us some of your time and some of your love.'

A sigh shook his chest. 'You and the baby have all my love. I may not be with you all the time but everything that I am is for you and our child.'

'That's more than enough.'

'Even if I work double shifts sometimes. If I come home tired and full of the weight of the day.'

'That's okay. You know it is.'

'I love you, Jess.'

'I love you too, Greg.'

For long moments they just smiled, the words echoing around them like a web of finely spun joy. Then she was on her feet. He moved at the same time, pulling her towards him and onto his lap, holding her tightly against his beating heart.

'How long is Charles going to be?' Jess was trying, without much success, to keep at least one strand of her attention on the door.

'We won't be interrupted. Charles makes an art out of discretion.'

'Well, you'd better kiss me, then. Quickly…'

He cut her short. Kissed her slowly, taking his time to savour it. 'I was wrong, Jess. I'm sorry.'

'I was wrong, too. And I'm sorry.'

He chuckled. 'You're going to fight me over it? I was wronger than you.'

She laughed, wrapping her arms around his neck. 'There's no such word as "*wronger*". We were both wrong. But we've got this chance now, and I'm not going to let it go.'

'I thought for a while that I'd left it too late. That you wouldn't come with me.'

'Yeah, so did I. But I was just kidding myself. There was no way I couldn't have come.'

He dropped a kiss onto her brow. 'No way I couldn't have asked you. Or kept on asking if you turned me down the first time.'

'I want to tell you something, Greg.' Jess pressed her lips together.

'Whatever it is, it doesn't matter.'

'No, it does. I'll say this now and then there's an end to it. We can leave it behind here.' She dug him gently in the ribs. 'I'm sure Charles knows what to do with any worn-out thoughts that people leave floating around in his office.'

He chuckled. 'No doubt he does. What do you want to say?'

Jess took a deep breath. 'I thought that I could do it all by myself, Greg. I'd told myself for so long that I didn't need my father, that I didn't care that he wasn't around, that I started believing it. I didn't want to feel that loss.'

'You feel it now?'

'Yeah. In a strange way I do. But you'll help me through that, won't you? You'll show me that there's a different way to make a family.'

'We'll face that together. We'll show each other, darling.' He hugged her tightly. 'I won't let you go, Jess. I'm not going to let you fall.'

'Mmm. I know. Feels good.' She took a moment to let the happiness seep a little further into her bones. Banishing the shadows. Freeing her from them. 'And you'll get to meet my mum and stepdad on Boxing Day. If you want to.'

'Of course I want to. Do you think they'll want to meet me?'

'My mum will love you. And I think you'll get on with

my stepdad too. They were going to help me move some furniture.'

'Right. Or I could do it for you and we could all sit down and have a nice meal. Get to know each other.'

'Or I could forget about moving the furniture and tell them I'm coming to live with you.'

He chuckled. 'That would be my first preference. Is there any particular reason why you want to move the furniture?'

'They want to help. I realised last week that I want them to help too.' She twined her fingers around his.

He chuckled. 'I'm sure you'll find something else for them to do. If you don't, I'll be sorting something out with your mother myself. But I'm glad you took that step.'

'Me too.'

'Will you take another?'

'I'm starting to get used to it. Why stop now?'

He kissed her. Warmly, tenderly and full of assurance now.

'Was that it?'

'No. I just did that because I wanted to. The step I want you to take is to sign these papers with me.'

'Me? Why me?'

'There's no legal requirement for you to sign them. But I want your name on there too. I want this to be something we do together.'

'Yes.' She could hardly wait to write her name under his. Help set him free.

'Then we'll go back to the hospital. Make sure that everyone's doing whatever it is they're supposed to be doing. Then I'll take you home and feed you.'

'You'll cook?' The thought of Greg's cooking was already making her stomach growl.

He chuckled. 'Yeah, I'll cook. And then...' He paused

just long enough for Jess to feel a shiver of expectation. 'And then I'll make love to you until you can't think straight, and you'll say yes to anything.'

'I can't think straight now.'

'Well, I'll make love to you anyway. That's the plan, and I'm going to stick to it.' His lips brushed her ear. 'When I slip that ring on your finger, I want it to be the only thing you're wearing.'

Jess couldn't answer. She didn't dare draw the inevitable conclusion and then be wrong. Perhaps it was some other ring.

'That okay with you?'

'Y-yes?' She gulped out the word.

His eyes reflected the concern on his face. 'Jess? I'm sorry, am I going too fast?'

She took a deep breath. 'No. I'm just not quite sure where you're going, that's all.'

'Ah. Okay, where was I?' He stopped to think for a moment. 'Yeah. Making love to you until you couldn't think straight.'

'Liking it so far.'

'Good. Then I hold you, tell you that I love you and ask you to marry me. And then you say…?'

'Yes?'

He smiled. 'That's exactly what you'll say. Then I'll put the ring on your finger.' He caught her left hand and brushed a kiss on her third finger. 'Seal the deal.'

She didn't need to answer. He saw it in her face. 'Two deals in one day.' The first gave Greg his life back. The second gave her everything she had ever wanted.

'I'll wait until midnight. At one minute past twelve on Christmas morning we'll have this Christmas and all the other Christmases yet to come to look forward to together.'

'I love you, Greg.' She hugged him tight. 'What made you do all this?'

'Don't laugh.'

'I won't.'

'It was a dream.' He shrugged. 'About the path I was on. How things would end up. Does that sound completely crazy?'

A small shiver began to travel downwards from the nape of her neck but dissipated in the warmth of his embrace. Jess wondered if his dream had been anything like the one she'd had, and dismissed the thought.

'Not really. Dreams are just our unconscious minds, telling us what we already know.'

He nodded. 'Then I guess it was just me. Telling myself what my life would be like if I let you go. And that I love you and our child more than anything.'

'That's all either of us needs to know.' She could let him go now. Now that she knew he wasn't going anywhere. And the sooner she did, the sooner he could sign the papers and they could be out of there. Jess slid off his lap and sat back in her own chair. 'By the way, have you got a turkey?'

'No. Have you?'

'I wasn't really banking on doing much celebrating.'

He sprang to his feet, suddenly full of energy, and strode towards the door, flinging it open and bellowing down the stairs. 'Charles…Charles, we need to sign the papers. And do you know where we can get a turkey? It's Christmas!'

* * * * *

Merry Christmas

& A Happy New Year!

Thank you for a wonderful 2013...

A sneaky peek at next month…

Medical Romance

CAPTIVATING MEDICAL DRAMA—WITH HEART

My wish list for next month's titles…

In stores from 3rd January 2014:

❑ *Her Hard to Resist Husband* – Tina Beckett

& *The Rebel Doc Who Stole Her Heart* – Susan Carlisle

❑ *From Duty to Daddy* – Sue MacKay

& *Changed by His Son's Smile* – Robin Gianna

❑ *Mr Right All Along* – Jennifer Taylor

& *Her Miracle Twins* – Margaret Barker

Available at WHSmith, Tesco, Asda, Eason, Amazon and Apple

Just can't wait?

Special Offers

Every month we put together collections and longer reads written by your favourite authors.

Here are some of next month's highlights— and don't miss our fabulous discount online!

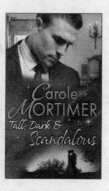

On sale 3rd January On sale 3rd January On sale 20th December

Save 20%
on all Special Releases

0114/ST/MB449

Work hard, play harder...

Welcome to the Gold Coast, where hearts are broken as quickly as they are healed. Featuring some of the rising stars of the medical world, this new four-book series dives headfirst into Surfer's Paradise.

Available as a bundle at
www.millsandboon.co.uk/medical

Join the Mills & Boon Book Club

> Want to read more **Medical** books?
> We're offering you **2 more** absolutely **FREE!**

We'll also treat you to these fabulous extras:

- Exclusive offers and much more!

- FREE home delivery

- FREE books and gifts with our special rewards scheme

Get your free books now!

visit **www.millsandboon.co.uk/bookclub**
or call Customer Relations on **020 8288 2888**